BETWEEN
WORLDS

BETWEEN WORLDS

IN CZECHOSLOVAKIA, ENGLAND, AND AMERICA

SUSAN GROAG BELL

for Dee, a comforting presence
at IRWG.

Susan Groag Bell
2/5/92

A WILLIAM ABRAHAMS BOOK

DUTTON

DUTTON

Published by the Penguin Group
Penguin Books USA Inc., 375 Hudson Street,
New York, New York 10014, U.S.A.
Penguin Books Ltd, 27 Wrights Lane, London W8 5TZ, England
Penguin Books Australia Ltd, Ringwood, Victoria, Australia
Penguin Books Canada Ltd, 2801 John Street,
Markham, Ontario, Canada L3R 1B4
Penguin Books (N.Z.) Ltd, 182-190 Wairau Road,
Auckland 10, New Zealand

Penguin Books Ltd, Registered Offices: Harmondsworth, Middlesex, England

First published by Dutton, an imprint of New American Library,
a division of Penguin Books USA Inc.

Distributed in Canada by McClelland & Stewart Inc.

First Printing, July, 1991
10 9 8 7 6 5 4 3 2 1

 REGISTERED TRADEMARK—MARCA REGISTRADA

LIBRARY OF CONGRESS CATALOGING-IN-PUBLICATION DATA:

Bell, Susan G.
  Between worlds : in Czechoslovakia, England, and America : a
memoir / by Susan Groag Bell.
    p.   cm.
  "A William Abrahams book."
  ISBN 0-525-93314-X
  1. Bell, Susan G. 2. Women historians—United States—Biography.
I. Title.
D15.B37A3   1991
907'.202—dc20   90-25796
                                                            CIP

Printed in the United States of America
Set in Galliard

Designed by Steven N. Stathakis

AUTHOR'S NOTE

Alma Campbell Kays (1923-1982) frequently urged me to record these memories. Many other friends, including Barbara Gelpi, Louise Freund, Lilian Furst, Stina Katchadourian, Wes Peverieri, Norris Pope, Nancy Roelker, Elizabeth Roden, Mollie Rosenhan, Michael Ryan, and Gabby Dpiegel, encouraged me in the early stages of writing, and I am grateful to all of them. Next, Marilyn Yalom's editorial pencil prodded me into loosening up and expanding the terseness of my account. Finally John Dean showed the manuscript to William Abrahams, who twitched his eyebrows, murmured a few suggestions and, magically, I knew how to transform a series of sketches into a book.

Palo Alto, 1990

CONTENTS

The following is an alphabetical list of German place names used in this book and their Czech equivalents.

GERMAN NAME	CZECH NAME
Brün	Brno
Grätz	Hradec nad Moravici
Jägerndorf	Krnov
Johannisbrunn	Jánské Koupele
Karlsbad	Karlovy Vary
Marienbad	Marianské Lázně
Meltsch	Melč
Olmütz	Olomouc
Ostrau	Ostrava
Stablowitz	Stablovice
Theresienstadt	Terezín
Troppau	Opava
Witkowitz	Vitkovice

BETWEEN WORLDS

PART I

CHILDHOOD
IN
CZECHOSLOVAKIA

CHAPTER

1

THE PHOTOGRAPH FOR which my mother won a prize has been part of my existence for as long as I can remember. It stood on my mother's desk and, later, accompanied her into exile and to a new life. It now graces my chest of drawers, where it attracts the attention of all who see it. It depicts my father, a large, comfortable, and relaxed figure, and myself, aged about three, sitting at an appetizingly arranged breakfast table in the bay window of our apartment. My father, wearing a dressing gown instead of a jacket over his shirt and tie, is obviously ready to leave for his office. He is smoking his after-breakfast cigarette and smiling at me, clad in pyjamas, across the curved, white Rosenthal coffeepot, the basket of rolls, butter, and honey.

The setting of this picture is roughly 1930 in the provincial town of Troppau, the capital of Silesia during the Austro-Hungarian Empire, known to history as the site of the 1820 Congress of Troppau, the follow-up to the Congress of Vienna. The town lies on the northern border of the new Czechoslovak republic, which was created in 1918, the decade before my birth. Ever since I was a small child and first saw a map of this country hanging on the classroom wall, I have thought of Czechoslovakia as a fish lying horizontally in the center of Europe. The fish's broad head is surrounded by Germany on the north and west and by Austria in the south. Poland runs along its northern flank, and Hungary and Rumania do the same in the south. The tip of the fish's slender tail abuts onto Russia. The town of Troppau was situated at the point where Czechoslovakia, Poland, and Germany met in the peripheral area encircling the western edge of the new republic. By the end of the decade, this troublesome area had become notorious as the Sudetenland, the pawn lifted from the Czech board and handed to Hitler for "peace in our time" by Great Britain's prime minister, Neville Chamberlain.

Troppau had been founded in the thirteenth century and, during my childhood, still had several well-kept fourteenth- and fifteenth-century churches and monastic medieval structures. Many other buildings were erected in the early eighteenth century in that unique late Baroque mixture of grand simplicity with touches of whimsicality. We lived in one of these.

Like the majority of the town's forty thousand inhabitants, my family spoke an Austrian variety of German, while the peasants living in the surrounding countryside spoke Czech. This followed a centuries-old pattern, unchanged during the old Habsburg Empire when the Austrian minority ruled over its far-flung subjects, including Czechs, Slovaks, Hungarians, Serbs, and many others. When, after the First World War, the town was incorporated into the new Czechoslovak republic under its liberator and philosopher-president Tomaš Masaryk, Czech was decreed as the official language to be used in government offices and courts of law. Prague became the national capital; its government attempted to make Czech the dominant language, and officially Troppau was now known by its Czech name: Opava. But such was the republic's tolerance that children could attend either the Czech or the German schools that coexisted in our town, provided that German-speaking children learned to speak and to write Czech in school, and indeed both languages were freely used. For example, I spoke German at home and attended German-speaking schools. But aged nine, I began to have Czech-language classes in my elementary school and my parents engaged a Czech woman known as "Slečna" (Miss) to converse with me in Czech two afternoons a week after I came home from school. Because of their Austrian heritage, however, German-speaking families, like ours, still considered Vienna rather than Prague their cultural capital. And so my mother and her friends occasionally journeyed to Vienna to visit the opera, to see the new plays, to buy new books, and to study the latest fashions by sitting in Viennese coffeehouses and watching the world go by.

But while people like my parents were interested in a purely cultural connection with the former Austrian regime, others never reconciled themselves to the rule of those they considered their ethnic inferiors. Centuries of enmity between Czechs and the Germans and Austrians who now were clustered in several pockets in and around the mountainous districts that formed the bone structure of the Czech fish's head were not easily swept away. A large majority of German-speaking citizens of the new Czechoslovak Republic chafed under what they thought of as the Czech yoke, and enmity flared into hatred during the worldwide depression of the early 1930s, when German-speaking citizens of the republic blamed the Czech government for the poverty that threatened their districts. When Hitler appeared on the European scene, these disaffected Czechoslovak citizens united under the term "Sudeten German" (after the local Sudeten mountain range) and formed a political party, which by 1937 had gained over 60 percent of the German vote in Czechoslovakia. The Sudeten Germans, under their leader Konrad Henlein, were eager to join the Third Reich. Unfortunately for my family and many of our friends, most of the population of Troppau belonged to this party.

An article in *The New York Times* about a painting by the Viennese secessionist painter Gustav Klimt has recently jolted my memory about this early period of my life. The article described a 1914 Klimt portrait that was expected to sell at auction for two to three million dollars. The sitter, the painter's patroness, Madame Primavesi, lived in a town near Troppau named Olmütz, where my family had close friends. The newspaper article, accompanied by a reproduction of Madame Primavesi's portrait in a flower-embellished Art Nouveau party dress, brought my mother's and grandmother's generations vividly to life. It unlocked successive submerged memories of my own childhood and the people, many now lost, who then formed my world, and quite suddenly I was impelled to recapture this world by writing about it. Those years have become blurred in my mind into a time before some cataclysmic event: a milestone that seems to have divided my life into a "before and after." In retrospect, I am aware that this cataclysm was the rise of Hitler and the nazification of central Europe.

I cannot be specific about what I remember of my earliest years. It astonishes me to read the positive and sharply defined early memories of certain autobiographers. Perhaps Darwin was right when he wrote that it is only those persons with powerful minds whose memories extend into their earliest years. And, like Darwin, I must admit that "this is not so in my case." My memories before the age of eight or nine are hazy and diffuse with only a generalized blur of people, highlighted by vivid splashes of certain events. I certainly do not remember the period of that photograph at the breakfast table when I was three or four, or anything else from this time that I do not suspect of having been told me by my parents, or absorbed by listening to others or by looking at the family photographs. Even more distressing than the lack of early memories of outside events, even those that affected me personally, is the complete absence of memories of my interior life. Edmund Gosse, for example, in his *Father and Son* tells us in the greatest detail of his mental struggles to comprehend complex ideas of morality (such as whether or not he was guilty of lying), his recognition of the fact that his father was not omniscient, and his disappointment when he discovered that Primrose Hill in London was not, in fact, covered with primroses—all at the age of five. The last of these three is perhaps the most easily attributable to a child of five. But not even such a simple and accessible childhood memory as the disappointment in finding that a name does not fit an object has remained with me.

I have pondered the reasons for my difficulties in remembering my early life very precisely, even to my inability to impose a chronological order on the years before my eleventh or twelfth. The reason that seems to make the most sense is that the unresolved shock of having so suddenly and drastically lost my stable home and many of the people who created it, on the eve of adolescence, has pushed these events into an unrecoverable haze of nostalgia.

The newspaper reproduction of that Klimt portrait of Madame Primavesi acted on me like a whiff of perfume or a few bars of music in conjuring up my mother's youth. It was not only the fact that my mother had been a young girl of fourteen when the portrait had been painted and that she had a particular admiration for Klimt's marvelously sinuous and sparkling figures. Her childhood home, which

I still remember very well, was on the Olmützerstrasse, the street leading out to Olmütz, where Klimt's patroness had lived. Moreover, the face of Klimt's patroness then, by extension, or perhaps through those strange contortions of memory that may or may not be true, reminded me of my mother's childhood friend, Resl Sonnenschein, who had lived in Olmütz.

My grandparents and the Sonnenscheins were of the same generation as the Primavesis: Resl's father a respected physician, my grandfather a local judge. Had my mother and Resl belonged to the manufacturing bourgeoisie instead of the professional classes, they might have become playmates of Madame Primavesi's little daughter, Mäda, whose stunning portrait, also painted by Klimt, and now in the Metropolitan Museum in New York, had already been sold in the 1930s to recoup "a series of financial reverses." My family and the Sonnenscheins had similar financial reverses in the 1930s, no doubt due to the same causes of economic depression and antisemitism. Unfortunately, neither family was in a position to sell Klimt portraits and transfer the money out of the country. Moreover, I cannot, by the wildest stretch of imagination, see my grandmother—a sad, drawn-looking woman—in Klimt's glorious mosaic colors. My grandfather, a very austere man, would have prevented her from bursting into exciting colors or excitement of any sort.

My own happiest memory of my grandparents' apartment, in which my mother lived until she married, was the bathroom with its enormous sunken marble bath. Three steps led down into this square tub, which was large enough for about three or four children to paddle about in. My grandmother indulgently allowed me and my friends to play in it whenever I visited her. Afterward she fed us a choice repast on her fluted white china decorated with bunches of violets.

Unfortunately, during most of my mother's growing up, my grandmother was quite ill. When she was sixteen, her eight-year-old brother, Fritz, became her responsibility while my grandmother spent many months in the hospital undergoing several serious operations. My grandfather considered himself the moral force of the household, possibly because his wife was so often ill, but perhaps because such was his nature. As a child and young girl, my mother thus lived in the shadow of an ailing mother and a severe father. It did not sound to me as though she had any fun. On one occasion, when she was about seventeen, in the midst of the First World War, she went to the park with her friend Grete Moller, chaperoned by the respectable Frau Moller, my grandparents' friend. The park was transformed from its usual provincial stillness by the noisy, colorful officers garrisoned in the town. The two young girls sat on a bench watching the excitement. After a bit, Grandfather came walking along on his way from the office and ordered his daughter to come home with him immediately, as he considered it unsuitable for a young girl to be sitting on a park bench.

Sometime in my sixth or seventh year, when she was in her fifties, my grandmother died and left me with an early memory of having to walk about the town, my hand clasped in that of my mother, whose hat embellished by a stylish black mourning veil caused me deep embarrassment.

Although I had known my mother's mother, her constant illnesses and finally her death had made me most uneasy, and my paternal grandmother had died long before I was born. However, by the time I was old enough to be aware of such things, Sofie, or Grandmama Feitzinger, while not my real grandmother, was a fixture in our household.

In fact Grandmama Feitzinger was already part of my life when I was six months old. There we both are, staring at the camera, in a sepia photograph, I sitting round and fat on her lap with enormous, happy brown eyes. Later, when our household moved into a couple of floors of the Palais Sobeck-Skal, Grandmama Feitzinger occupied one of the best large, square rooms overlooking the garden, with its own entrance and two pairs of deep double doors connecting her apartment to our drawing room. Grandmama Feitzinger made up for the loss of my real grandmothers. She was ever ready to entertain me with sausages, cookies, or chocolates, and her large green parrot greeted me courteously as soon as I appeared in her quarters. She read to me and told me interminable stories, often sat with me in the garden playing word games, or took me to the park to please us both. When one of our playmates asked us to explain this mysterious person, my friend Hanni described her as follows: "Grandmama Feitzinger is very old, she is a man, and she has a mustache and smokes cigars."

The Feitzinger family owned one of my favorite specialty shops, a stationer's, run by Grandmama's nephews Christian and Martin. This was where we bought all my school equipment, pens and pencils, notebooks, rulers, compasses, and so on. Occasionally Grandmama and I made our way to this paradise, where I was allowed to choose some crayons, a special pencil, or a notebook as a gift. Feitzinger's also sold all sorts of wonderful wrapping paper, and the greatest gift Grandmama Feitzinger ever bestowed upon me was a bundle of huge rolls of heavy, shiny gray-green paper to cover all my books. She taught me exactly how to do it, and I have never lost the art. I spent blissful afternoons carefully covering my books, proudly displaying particularly obstreperous large volumes to my parents, their friends, the servants, and anyone else whom I could bully into admiring my handiwork. There they stood on my shelves, uniformly and beautifully covered in gray-green, with their titles neatly written on their spines by my mother in the violet ink she always used.

But the best part of Grandmama Feitzinger's life with us was that she and my mother used to get together and tell me stories of my father's past. It was through them that I learned most of what I know about him. Thus I heard that, when my mother married my father in 1924, he was forty-eight and she twenty-four. People used to tease her, saying that he would always be twice her age, that by the time she was forty, he would be eighty, and that when she was fifty, he would be a hundred. This did not deter her, and alas, by the time she was forty, he had already lost his life in the concentration camp at Theresienstadt.

His family lived in the Austrian part of Silesia in Witkowitz, where my grandfather owned a granary near the coal (and now steel) town of Ostrau, or as the Czechs call it: Ostrava. The emperor, Franz-Joseph, had offered this grandfather a baronetcy for his distinguished part in feeding the army during the First World War, but he had refused to accept it. When my mother told me this romantic story, I had great difficulty in understanding why anyone should not want to be called "Herr Baron." Later, when I learned how difficult it was to keep up an aristocratic title and estates in a democratic republic, I found my grandfather's attitude rather sensible and less obscure.

My father was the youngest of nine children. Grandmama Feitzinger gave a little snort as she recounted that when he was old enough to understand flattery, in the early 1880s, his hair still hung to his shoulders in golden curls. Once he heard one of his mother's friends say to her, "Comme il est beau!" Thereafter he referred to himself with a wicked grin in his version of the French as "Hizhebo."

As a law student at the University of Vienna, my father enjoyed the delights of that city in the 1890s. He was, and remained, a bon vivant. About twenty years after he died,

I once found myself in a small student haunt, the Café Vienna in Berkeley, California, where the proprietress asked how it came about that I pronounced the word *Apfelstrudel* with the correct accent. When I told her the name of my hometown, she asked hesitantly whether I had ever heard of a lawyer in Troppau named Groag. "He was my father," I replied. She completely lost her head and rushed to the old man sitting at the cash desk, crying, "Otto, Otto, you will never guess who is here." Otto turned out to be my father's cousin, with whom he had lived during his student days in Vienna. After the first excitement was over, Otto proceeded to tell his favorite story of how he and my father had found themselves without money in a Vienna coffeehouse and how my father had left him there as a hostage while he went to search for the necessary funds.

With his new law degree, my father set up his practice, a few miles from his home in Ostrau, in the nearby town of Troppau, where his oldest sister, Anna, had married a physician. He had more or less established himself when, in 1914, the war broke out. In due course he joined the Austrian army and, captured by the Russians, soon found himself interned as a prisoner in Siberia, where he sat out the remainder of the war. My father loved mountains, lakes, and trees; in fact, he spent much of his time walking in the most beautiful natural environments he could find. But he hated birches. He used to insist that, having been surrounded by them in his Siberian prison camp, the very sight of their graceful white stems made him feel ill.

Because the revolution was in full spate in western Russia, when the war was ended in 1918, he returned to Europe with a shipload of other captured Austrian officers via China, San Francisco, and the Panama Canal. He spoke seldom of this period, but friends who enjoyed his imperturbability reported that he was in the middle of a game of bridge when they reached the isthmus. Everyone else wanted to stand at the railings and look at the canal, but he insisted that the famous sight would wait and they should first finish the rubber.

Returning to Troppau in the newly formed Czechoslovak republic, and having lost his former practice because of the war, he was forced to reorganize his life. He took some rooms in the law office of the man who was to become his father-in-law and my grandfather. There he eventually met my mother, who assisted her father by taking briefs to court and serving as a law clerk.

At this time, my father made his home in a couple of rooms in the apartment of an elderly lady who treated him like a son. She was Sofie Feitzinger, who in due course became a de facto member of our family and my surrogate grandmama. When my father announced to Sofie Feitzinger that he intended to marry my mother, he encountered heavy resistance. Sofie did not want him to leave. Finally they compromised. It was arranged that as long as she wished, she should live in my parents' home; and that is exactly what happened.

In the middle of the 1930s, when I was about eight, I began to notice that Grandmama Feitzinger was easily tired and less eager to entertain me. One day, when I came into her sunny room, she was sitting on the side of her bed and seemed to have difficulty in dressing herself. I was deeply shocked to see her pendulous old woman's breasts, so different from the firm bosom of my mother. Grandmama sent me to ask my mother to come in to see her. I ran out of the room, only too glad to do so. Soon after this, she moved away from us, to stay with her nephews, I was told. A few weeks later she was dead.

While my father and I used to sit at the small table in the bay in front of the drawing room balcony, he drinking his breakfast coffee and I my chocolate, my mother breakfasted in bed. Afterwards, when he had left for his law office in the Wagnergasse, my mother consulted the cook about the meals for the next two days.

After the menu discussion, my mother made her toilette; during vacations and weekends I kept her company. I enjoyed helping her decide what to wear and watching her cosmetic routine in front of the floor-length oval mirror between the two long windows overlooking the garden. On Sunday mornings Herr Huppert came to pedicure my parents' feet. While he worked on my mother, my father usually took a bath, and if I wandered into the bathroom where he lay soaking in the tub, he chatted with me about this and that, always with a washcloth neatly draped over the lower part of his body. Why didn't my mother object to my seeing her naked while my father kept himself covered? I never asked them to explain.

Midmorning it was the custom to eat a small collation known as *Gabelfrühstück*, literally a "fork-breakfast," which the English call "elevenses," and the Americans have reduced to midmorning coffee. The *Gabelfrühstück* was a comforting sort of meal. Sometime in the 1930s my mother developed a duodenal ulcer, and Doctor Burckhardt encouraged her to eat the yolks, but not the whites, of eggs as part of her diet. Thus, every morning at ten o'clock, for a number of years, she was served a soft-boiled egg in a blue-and-white egg cup. She sat at the table with my dog, Struppel, on the floor at her right, and Kostja, our black cat, at her left. She ate the egg yolk with a roll and butter and alternately dropped pieces of the egg white to the two expectant animals, who snapped them up greedily.

On weekday mornings when I was not at school, I accompanied her shopping to numerous specialty stores for meat, fish, delicatessen, groceries, and greengroceries. The only thing she did not buy in stores was the milk, which was delivered every morning on a horse-drawn cart, from which the maids collected it in large red enamel jugs. In the summer, the iceman delivered huge blocks of ice that were stowed in a deep bench-chest in the kitchen. After shopping for food, my mother made her way to the pharmacy of her oldest childhood friend, Grete Moller. This store provided a daily meeting place with my father, and they then returned home together for lunch.

Sometimes in the afternoon I went with my mother to her dressmaker, Madame Filbert, who had a salon above a coffeehouse, in the corner building of our street, where the Herrengasse crossed the Töpfergasse. From its windows, while the women discussed the latest creations and my mother had her fittings, I watched the people going about their business in this part of town. Only once was Madame Filbert required to make clothes for me—a very special pink taffeta birthday dress—as my own clothes were normally sewn by Fräulein Schmidt, who came to the house and also mended the linen. Together Madame Filbert and my mother concocted some splendid garments, and my mother, who had a flair for elegance, was often entreated to allow her designs to be copied. On a certain occasion, the Baroness Ina Sobeck-Skal lusted after one of my mother's particularly exotic frocks. It was a tightly fitting pale gray silk with small rose-colored flowers, unbelted with a flared collar surrounding a vee neck. Innumerable tiny buttons, covered with the same material, closed the dress from her breast to the knees. My mother, who was tall and slim and carried herself with exceptional grace, looked stunning in this dress, which she designed when I was about ten years old. With her agreement, Madame Filbert made an exact replica for the Baroness Ina. Even I could see that the baroness's lack of height and voluptuous curves did not produce the same effect.

Often on weekday afternoons my mother's friends came to tea and were closeted with her in her private sitting room, where I joined them when I returned from school. I considered all of these men and women as my friends. The beautiful and elegant milliner Grete Schoenberger had an intriguing shop where she created dashing wide-brimmed hats. Frieda Troester owned a smart little black wire-haired dachshund named Lumpi and inspired us to acquire my tan-colored Struppel of the same breed. Various unattached menfriends of my mother's were the best companions as far as I was concerned, as they were most willing to play my favorite games. I remember hours of Mah-jongg and pickup-sticks, which we called Mikado, and occasionally we aspired to a simple game of chess. The reclusive Franz-Josef Häusler, who was usually brought in to escort Tante Resl during her Troppau visits, was one of these accommodating bachelors; another was Baron Bayer von Bayersburg, who lived on his estates outside the town and drove in occasionally to see my mother.

On weekdays during the summer we often went to the public swimming pool. This was a well-designed place, practically in the country at the other end of the tram line, with shops, a restaurant, and small apartments for changing. My friends and I climbed all over a monstrous concrete sculpture of a giant with bulging eyes who guarded the edge of the pool, which was large and never crowded. My mother lounged for hours in a deck chair, chatting to friends or reading, while I played in the water with my companions. On alternative summer afternoons we visited one of the two open-air cafés in the town park. There, to the strains of a string orchestra, the grownups, including my mother, danced, while I indulged in vanilla or coffee ice cream, served with wafers, in small metal dishes with straight-lipped spoons.

Sometimes, after school, my mother and I went to the new children's lending library, which had opened like a dream or an answer to my prayers. I had long since exhausted the space on my bookshelves, and my parents and their friends found it difficult to satisfy my voracious reading habits. Most of my collection I knew by heart, having read and re-read them endlessly. When I was seven, I contracted scarlet fever with complications and horrid pains in the middle ear, and soon after that Dr. Burckhardt decided that my appendix should be removed. Throughout the week I spent there after the operation, my mother stayed with me in the room in the small clinic. During these and other minor children's ailments, my mother read aloud to me for hours on end. She never seemed to tire of the repetitions of *Dr. Doolittle* and Karen Michaelis's *Bibi* (the adventures of a Danish girl), all in multiple volumes, which were my greatest treasures. Most of these favorite books had been brought to me by my father when he returned from his solitary vacations in the mountains, or from business trips to Prague, Vienna, or Berlin. I used to look forward with unparalleled excitement to his return, knowing that he would satisfy my great desire not only for his comforting presence but also for books. The most wonderful present he ever bestowed on me was on Easter Sunday morning when I was eleven. He called me into his study and told me that he had hidden for me something that I should look for in a sort of Easter egg hunt. I scrambled about his desk and innumerable papers and finally, among the cushions of his sofa, discovered a little box with my name on it in which I found a splendid tomato-red fountain pen. "There," he said. "Instead of reading all those books, perhaps you will write one." I was delighted with this treasure, with its golden nib, which I used happily until I was in my twenties, when alas it could no longer be repaired.

My mother presented a more disturbing presence than my father—I was never sure that I had come up to her expectations and quite often feared her anger. When, on my return from school, there were no visitors in the house,

I used to find her curled up with a book, sharing her sitting-room couch with our animals. After reporting on my achievements at school that day, we would have a little game of Double Patience before tea. One miserable afternoon each week, however, was devoted to accounts. This was the most uncomfortable half-hour and has left me with a horror of double-entry bookkeeping. I received a tiny allowance of a few *Kronen* and was expected to keep careful records of my spending in a small green notebook. Try as I would, I never managed to balance the account. This had nothing to do with my ability at mathematics. In fact my school arithmetic was always faultless. But my mother's stern face, expecting me to produce the perfect statement, unnerved me to such an extent that I could not bring myself even to prepare for the accounting and usually arrived with a few hasty figures scratched into the pristine columns. The session invariably ended with a scolding and exhortations to perform better next week. I never did. My mother, however, earned her living as a tax accountant for thirty years, after her life as a lady of leisure had been dramatically brought to an end by the Nazi regime.

Sometimes she told me stories of her own childhood and her life at her parents' home. When she was very young, she spent her summers on the farm of her grandparents Mandl outside Brünn, which the Czechs call Brno, in Moravia. I was able to remember something of my lessons of biology and heredity because early on I was made aware that Abbot Gregor Mendel, whose name was so similar to that of my great-grandparents, did his "Mendelian" experiments in the garden of his monastery in Brünn.

After her childhood summer vacations, my mother and grandmother returned to Troppau, where my grandfather awaited them impatiently in their apartment in the Olmützerstrasse. They always arrived from the farm laden with fruit, vegetables, fish, and fowl. A favorite story that

I insisted on being told over and over again when I was small, and perhaps not so small, was how once, on her return to town, my mother stole a chicken that the cook had put on the windowsill ready for plucking. She then wrapped it in a shawl and spirited it into the courtyard garden behind the house, where she regaled it with fairy tales. I also had a vivid picture of the irate scolding she received from their red-faced cook, who hunted high and low for the chicken in order to prepare it for the pot.

Perhaps as a result of the austerity of her upbringing and as a reaction to her father's sternness, my mother began to indulge in the good life after her marriage and never stinted herself or me in the pleasures of the flesh. All the same, she inherited her father's firm adherence to principles and, in some ways, his severity. Honesty and obedience were her moral foundation and her rules for me. Her formal religious education as a child was that of a Jewish liberal. When she married my father, who had decided to become officially assimilated as a Protestant, she also took instruction from the Protestant minister, Pfarrer Herr. He told her that her religious childhood education by the local rabbi had already more than adequately prepared her for his brand of Lutheranism. As she related it later, these two religious leaders of our town understood each other very well on most theological issues. We never discussed the reasons for my parents' change of religion, but it was my implicit understanding that since genuine faith was absent it was more a matter of belonging to a certain social group. In the Habsburg Empire, and perhaps in most of the Western world, every official personal document had to be completed with the individual's religious affiliation. I later surmised that my parents felt that the religious group they were forced to declare might as well be one without the centuries-old social stigma that was attached to the Hebrew religion. And so, like millions of others who had been brought up as Jews, they changed to one of the more common Christian religious communities. I was baptized soon after my birth and as a small child sent to the Lutheran pastor for the biblical instruction that is necessary to make one a literate member of Judeo-Christian society.

The majority of the population in our town, however, was Catholic. When I reached primary school age, my parents opted against the Catholic parish school run by nuns, in whose district we lived, and sent me two miles farther to the secular elementary school, the Rossischule, where I had a free period when the Catholic priest offered religious instruction. My friend Hanni and I then wandered off to play, and on weekends I went to the Lutheran Sunday school and she to the rabbi. Our heretic status notwithstanding, when we were a little older the Catholic girls in our school relied on Hanni's and my help with their religious observance. They had a problem with thinking of enough sins to confess to the priest on Saturdays. And so, on Friday afternoons a group of us used to get into a huddle on the playground or in a deserted classroom, and Hanni and I brought our imaginations to bear on possible sins that might satisfy a priest looking for the misdeeds of innocent girls. Our heretical inventions must have been adequate, as we were repeatedly invited to help in this deception of the Catholic church by its small parishioners. Hanni and I later wondered whether the priest was surprised at the sudden improvement in these girls' morals after we were no longer at their school.

Neither of my parents attended church, but one of our maids was detailed to escort and collect me to and from the Protestant service every Sunday morning. I much preferred to sneak with the Catholic maids into the Church of the Holy Ghost opposite our house. Here the flowing baroque shapes and glowing colors, the scents and music,

were far more intriguing than the austere and simple cere-
mony in Pfarrer Herr's redbrick Lutheran church at the
other end of the park.

On my return from church on Sundays, I sometimes
joined my parents at the restaurant, just behind our house
in the Sperrgasse, where they and their friends had gathered
for a preluncheon drink. But as my mother did not enjoy
either beer or wine, this did not happen very often. Instead,
I accompanied one of the maids to the restaurant to bring
home a foaming glass of beer for my father to drink with
his lunch.

Our meals were served at the round mahogany table
in the dining room. As we finished, there was a small ritual.
My mother stood with her hand on the bellpull that hung
from the chandelier above the table, ready to ring for the
maid to clear the dishes. While she stood thus, my father
kissed her forehead, her eyes, and lastly her mouth. Once,
for a few days, maybe a week, they were angry with each
other. I did not know the cause, but was deeply disturbed
when the kissing ritual did not take place. Finally, I could
bear it no longer and pushed my parents together until
laughingly they performed to my satisfaction.

My parents believed that the best recipe for a happy
marriage and good family life was to have as much privacy
and as little forced togetherness as possible. For example,
as soon as space allowed, quite early in their marriage, they
had separate bedrooms. In the same vein, they often had
separate vacations. While they had many interests in common, each also had specific preferences that the other could
live without.

My mother loved opera and theater and would happily
spend many evenings sitting in their box at the Troppauer
town theater. My father was known to nod off at the opera,
particularly during Wagnerian performances. So she was

often escorted by various family friends, while he settled down to a game of bridge at one of the local coffeehouses.

Once every winter my mother went to Vienna for two or three weeks, where, in the company of our Viennese friends Karl and Steffi Fried, she enjoyed the rich cultural life of a capital city. Karl was my father's second cousin and had been his fellow student at the university. Both Frieds, whom I adored, were attorneys, Steffi being an early example of a woman who, in her late thirties, studied for the bar, after she had been married for quite a while. Sometimes other friends accompanied my mother during these Viennese visits. She always returned home to our provincial city with a new lease on life and full of the latest ideas in books, art, fashion, and gossip. One of the first things my mother did on her return was to take pages from the latest Viennese fashion magazines to her dressmaker, Madame Filbert, to suggest styles for her new wardrobe.

My father's separate vacations were of another sort. He usually went off in the late spring or early autumn to Karlsbad or Marienbad or some other spa, where he bathed, drank the waters, enjoyed extensive walks in the mountains, and played bridge with the other guests. When I met his cousin Otto—by then in his eighties in Berkeley, California—I had the unnerving experience of hearing how on one of these occasions in Marienbad, my father had proudly showed him photographs of myself as a nine-month-old baby.

Frequently also, my parents went together to one of the splendidly situated hotels and spas in the Czech or Austrian mountains. Among my earliest memories, whether my own or one impressed on me by my mother, is of reciting a poem entitled *Die Rehlein*, about young deer, as my parents stepped into the house on their return from one of these vacations.

At least once a year I joined my parents at some resort.

Usually this was Johannisbrunn, a place not too far from Troppau. I loved Johannisbrunn, where we were well known at the *Kurhotel*. The best part of these holidays was the early morning. As at home, my mother either did without breakfast or had it served in our room, while my father and I went for a walk in the forest. How sad it is that, unlike so many people who remember details of their mental development, I remember nothing of what he and I talked about on these occasions. I do, however, remember the most wonderful breakfasts following those early morning walks, on the hotel terrace overlooking the mountains. Never since, however much I have tried to simulate the exact circumstances, have newly baked crisp rolls with sweet butter and honey tasted quite as delicious as they did on those fresh and scented summer mornings in the open air.

Our days at Johannisbrunn were taken up with walks in the forest, swims in the pool cut out of the river where we lay or played on the banks, and, to my mind, exotic meals in the hotel's grand dining room. Spa hotels in central Europe were located in carefully chosen scenic areas, with landscaped avenues for walking. Strategically placed benches overlooked the best views at intervals. While the swimming and playing at the river pool remain only a hazy but rather noisy blur, the forest walks are etched deeply in my memory. The spring from which Johannisbrunn took its name opened into a small stream that flowed through the forest, cascading over clean white stones, until it widened into the river with its pool close to the hotel. Pine, fir, and larch forests, with light sparkling through the branches, and clearings of logs and young trees offered both mystery and welcoming opportunities for play, for reading, and for quiet discoveries. The feel of brown sun-warmed needles below one's bare feet and the perfume of sun-drenched pines, occasionally mixed with the scent of blueberries, are memories that stab unguarded moments throughout life. No English woods, however beautiful, could replace these pine forests of Czechoslovakia, but the redwood grove below the bedroom I was lucky enough to sleep in for twenty years in California came close to recreating one of the most comforting memories of my childhood.

One of the great pleasures of those hotel vacations was that the personnel was always the same. Nowadays the staff of most institutions appears to change not merely annually, but even with the season. The hotel at Johannisbrunn employed the same clerks, waiters, and chambermaids, who recognized me from one year to the next. The waiters indulgently allowed me to help them set the tables for the evening meals and taught me to fold napkins that sat up like rabbits on the plates. As a result, I took a proprietary interest in the hotel dining room with its grand chandeliers and splendid flower arrangements.

During my parents' vacations, I was sometimes also left in charge of the maids, who offered all kinds of entertainment not exactly pleasing to my parents. The activities of our cook Bertha, a dazzling blonde, caused quite a stir. One night while my mother was in Vienna, my father came home and caught Bertha entertaining a man friend rather too intimately in her bedroom.

The cook's bedroom was immediately underneath the bathroom, which had been created out of another ancient chamber in the grand old eighteenth-century palais in which we lived. The bathroom was large and spacious and was connected by a dumbwaiter to the cook's bedroom below. As her room was next to the kitchen, it was easy for her to send up dishes and food from the kitchen to the bathroom and thence to the dining room on the upper floor of our apartment. The dumbwaiter was large enough for my friends and me to curl up and creep into, and often, against the express commands of my mother, we pulled each other up and down. It was obviously easy to hear voices in the cook's bedroom through the lift when one was in the bath-room up above. Next to the cook's bedroom a wooden spiral staircase wound its way to a small landing that opened out just beside my bedroom. I remember my father marching down those spiral stairs on the occasion when, through the dumbwaiter, he heard the cook Bertha speaking to her lover. I also remember that night as the only time I heard my father raise his voice.

Of course, there was that other time, while my mother was in Vienna, when Bertha had taken me to the cinema against my father's expressed wishes. We had enjoyed a film with the famous actress Franziska Gaal, in which she played the part of a young woman whose mother wanted to hide her age from an admirer. When the mother's admirer arrived at the house and found the daughter standing behind the piano, looking all of her twenty years, the young woman snatched up a pair of scissors and quickly cut off the hem of her dress above the knee, appearing as the child her mother wanted her to be. I was excited and spellbound by the shortening of the dress, but my father strongly disapproved of my thinking about the theme behind this quick-witted maneuver and sternly reprimanded Bertha. By the time Bertha entertained her lover underneath my bedroom, she obviously had to go, and Rosa took her place.

I adored Rosa, the new cook, not only for what she produced in our kitchen, especially her plum and blueberry tarts, but for her love of fun and for her romantic and exciting village home, where I spent several summers. The village was Meltsch, about six miles from Troppau. It consisted of a partly ruined castle, inhabited by a mysterious old lady who always dressed in white; a church, which I later discovered to be the design of a famous modern architect; and a village street with a couple of shops. A wonderfully clear small stream, cascading over rocks and stones, led through the village to the castle. Rosa's father was the village blacksmith; her sister was married to the village baker. Both the forge and the bakeshop were deeply fascinating.

In Rosa's parents' house I slept, together with her, in a bed that was a sort of cupboard whose doors opened into the kitchen. This meant that while lying in bed one could watch all the family goings on, because the kitchen was in fact the main room of the house. We slept under a huge red featherbed comforter that was left to hang over the windowsill to air every morning. In the evenings when I was already in bed, the family sat around the kitchen table until it was time to sleep. The next morning they reappeared with the dawn. I was expected to rise at the same time and was given the intriguing job of feeding the pigs and chickens. In the evenings I was allowed to collect the eggs in a large basket. All remnants of food went to the pigs, and I became quite skillful at avoiding the larger sows when they chased their little piglets around the muddy yard. I could never understand why, by the time I came next year, there were different sows from the ones I had befriended before. Interestingly, although I became part of the village community during the summer, since I was not there in November, during the slaughter, the more painful parts of pig-keeping were not divulged.

I spent many afternoons in the Meltsch bakery. The perfume of baking bread is one of the most intoxicating and unforgettable scents I know. I would have been drawn to it in any case, as I was to the various bakeries at home, from which I used to collect the bread with Rosa twice weekly. The bread in Meltsch was as beautiful and delicious as the best bread we bought in town. Rosa's brother-in-law baked huge, only slightly raised round loaves at least a foot in diameter. They were made of rye flour, and their shiny brown crust, the glowing color of horse chestnuts, was ridged with equidistant narrow circles. Rosa and her family used to hold these loaves under one arm while cutting slices with sharp, thin knives. The bread, eaten with sweet butter or pork drippings and salt, tasted as good as it looked and smelled. Another product of Rosa's brother-in-law were his wonderful hard-crusted white rolls, which we had as treats on Sundays.

There was, however, a reason beyond the delights of fresh bread that attracted me to the bakery. While her brother-in-law produced bread, Rosa's sister produced babies. She was quite willing for me to look after her latest baby for hours on end. Some of my mother's friends had babies whom I was allowed to inspect only from afar. Rosa's sister's babies were entrusted to me for changing, for holding on my lap, and for pushing through the village in their carriages. Sometimes I spent long afternoons playing with them on the grass in the garden behind the bakery. As with the pigs, I became skillful at these various tasks and felt proud of myself when I could rock or sing a recalcitrant baby to sleep. The only place where I was not allowed to take the babies was into the forge.

Rosa's father's forge was naturally one of the other major attractions of these summers. It was only a few steps across the yard behind the family's living quarters. One or two horses usually stood around, waiting to be shod. The air was hot and dusty with sparks flying about, and as soon as one walked in the eye focused on a kaleidoscope of orange and crimson molten iron. The blacksmith himself was a comfortable large man with a booming voice to counteract the clashing and hammering of his forge. Like his daughters, he was willing for me to be part of the family and did not object to my hovering about the place or to my asking foolish questions of himself or his customers. One of the latter was a local farmer, with a daughter of my age, and she and I became friends and often spent our time wandering about the village together.

One afternoon we were invited to visit the lady who lived in the castle. She was alone in a room filled with books and sat in a deep chair, her long white dress draped over the footstool in front of her. She told us that she had known Rosa since Rosa had been a little girl of my age. She asked me all kinds of questions about my parents and my life at home. Then she showed us paintings and statues of her ancestors in some of the rooms of the castle. Finally she sent us out to one of her meadows, where she gave us carte blanche to eat as many raspberries as we wished and said we could return to the meadow whenever we liked. This meadow has remained my ideal meadow for all time. It curved into a range of pine trees at the rear and was surrounded by raspberry and blackberry hedges on the three other sides. A small gate in one side led to the castle garden. We made ourselves comfortable in the grass, told each other stories, and from time to time picked handfuls of raspberries.

One year my parents decided that I needed a change to something more sophisticated during the summer. One of the maids sewed nametapes into my clothes, and I was sent off, for two weeks, to a girls' camp in the grandly beautiful Slovakian Tatra mountains. The camp was run strictly and rigorously. We were expected to eat, play, and exercise routinely. All letters home to our parents had to be vetted by the director, a severe woman, who nevertheless allowed some freedom to the older girls. The afternoons were to be spent at a local café, where, under the supervision of these older girls, we could order ice cream and listen to the romantic thé-dansant orchestra. The two girls in charge of me giggled endlessly about things that were apparently unsuitable for me to share. They were passionately attached to the famous tenor Richard Tauber who was expected to appear in person during the week I was there. They practiced his theme song, *"Du bist mein ganzes Herz"*

(You are my heart's delight), until they seemed to have sucked all the music out of it.

After three days in this place, I decided I simply could not stand it. I smuggled a letter to my parents through one of the housemaids telling them how much I hated it. Then I tried to make the best of the situation by finding some nice companions. On the Saturday morning, after I had been there a week, I looked up from the garden bench where we were sitting and saw the most wonderful sight. My father was standing in the gateway. I ran to him through the flowerbeds and threw myself into his arms. He said simply, "I have come to take you home."

CHAPTER

2

Home, in those days, by a great piece of good luck was a wonderful place. All my friends remember it with awe and delight. We had moved into this house in 1933, the year that Hitler became chancellor of Germany and began to play a major role in international politics. I am sure that this fact did not trouble me at the time. I wonder, even, if my parents were much concerned by it. The move to our new house must, however, have made a deep impression on me for it was like no other house of my acquaintance. Nevertheless, I cannot remember my first reaction to it or even the great event of the move itself. It is as though I had lived in it forever and spent my entire childhood in this wonderful building. This house in which we now lived belonged to the Baron Sobeck-Skal, who was a member of one of innumerable impoverished minor aristocratic families that abounded in the greater Austro-Hungarian Empire. The baron owed my attorney father a great deal of money for his legal services. In a sort of barter system, we therefore lived rent-free in a splendid apartment that occupied most of two floors of the Sobeck-Skals' baroque townhouse.

The "Palais" Sobeck-Skal, as it is called in the guide books, was built in the Herrengasse, the Lords' Street, in the 1730s. One entered by a magnificent front portal that led into the porte cochere, a corridor within the house, through which at one time carriages, and now motorcars, drove into a courtyard and garden behind and thence into a back street. The baron had a pied-à-terre on one side of the front portal on the ground floor; the concierge lived in a couple of rooms on the other side. Two of the baron's maiden aunts and their four Pekingese dogs lived on the third floor under the mansard roof. Our apartment consisted of the spacious middle floor as well as the original eighteenth-century kitchen and servants' quarters at the back of the house on the ground floor. Our front windows overlooked the baroque Church of the Holy Ghost; our rear view was onto the comfortable courtyard with an ancient pump in the center and the quiet garden beyond.

I have many different memories of this great house, but perhaps the most asthetically and physically satisfying is the memory of the stoves that graced each of our rooms. These stoves reached almost to the ceiling, and they were slender and stately and completely covered with lustrous ceramic tiles. In my bedroom the tiles were a soft green; in the dining room a creamy white; in my parents' bedroom a dark wine red; and in the drawing room a rich dark blue. The stoves were wonderfully warm to the touch and gave out a comforting even heat that was neither too dry nor too moist. If one opened their small square doors, one could see the glowing embers, but this was not as important as the tall warm sentinel-like presence they bestowed upon the rooms they guarded. If I shut my eyes now, I can still feel the smooth warmth of their tiles against the palms of my hands. Halfway up each stove was a small hollow space covered with an ornamental grille in which one could place a coffeepot or some dish that needed to be kept warm throughout the day or night.

The Baron Victoren von Sobeck-Skal, who owned this house, was a tall, desiccated, and sad-looking man. The Baroness Ina, his wife, made up for this with her voluptuous, dark beauty, richly colored outré clothes, and the large tan boxer who was always at her side. Baroness Ina was a Russian whom the baron had rescued during the revolution. She spoke often of her "soul" in a deep rasping voice that reminded me of hazelnut cake with whipped cream. She also had a passionate admiration for the late Empress Elisabeth of Austria. They had no children of their own, but had adopted the baroness's "nephew," Bubi, who had long golden curls and was about my age. Bubi was an enigma. There was something puzzling about his background and his relationship to the baroness, but I never discovered what it was. The baroness usually arrived at the palais in a long low-slung car driven by her dashing young cousin Pitz Rollsberg, who charged after her in his ankle-length brown leather coat. Then, after she had settled into the pied-à-terre downstairs, she and Pitz came to have tea or liqueurs with my mother. They sat in the brown leather sofa and deep armchairs in our drawing room and all smoked cigarettes in long ivory holders.

The Sobeck-Skals owned two hunting lodges about ten miles out in the country. The baroness divided her time between one of these (while her husband was in the other), her little flat in Vienna, and the occasional night in the pied-à-terre below us. She was always eager for me to visit them in their country house in order that I might keep Bubi company. These occasions were wonderful and mysterious.

The first time I stayed in the hunting lodge in Stablowitz I must have been nine or ten. I had arrived fairly late in the evening. After an undistinguished supper, Bubi and I had a little swim in the large round carp pool in the middle of the garden. We chased around a bit and then were called in to go to bed. In order to make me feel at home, I had been given a small room next to the baroness's bedroom.

When I had settled into bed, the baroness came to say good night and to see that I had everything I needed. As usual, the boxer trotted by her side. Her dark hair was hanging loosely down her back and a floor-length open black velvet cape was draped over her shoulders—otherwise she was entirely naked. I had seen mature women's bodies. My mother was no prude and wandered about her bedroom quite unconcernedly without her clothes in my presence. Yet the Baroness Ina's nakedness hit me like a punch in the stomach. Perched on the side of my bed, she asked if I would like her to read to me, and, when I agreed delightedly, she began to read some incomprehensible Russian book. Bubi told me later that she was at that time deeply devoted to Dostoevsky, so I suppose it may have been one of his novels.

Later in the night I woke from a frightening dream and, hearing my restlessness, she called me in to chat with her. I went hesitantly through the connecting door and found her reading in bed. Her bedroom was dimly lit by three skulls in which small candles had been placed. Their light illuminated a silver crucifix on the wall behind the bed. The baroness was reclining in the bed with the boxer lying on a white fur rug by her side. She beckoned me to her bed, and I wondered where I should place myself. Finally I snuggled down on the rug with the dog.

The range of my childhood playmates ran the gamut from the aristocratic Bubi Sobeck-Skal to Ilse, a concierge's daughter. My parents were no snobs, and it never occurred to me that there was any social difference among the diverse children who were my companions.

My closest friend of that time, and the only one who

remained part of my life into adulthood, was Hanni Nath. We were pushed around the town park in our perambulators by our respective nannies. The German word for nanny, *Kinderfräulein*, has quite a different texture from the comforting image conjured up by the nanny of English lore. But perhaps it is only the title that appears so stilted. The person herself, whether Kinderfräulein or nanny, was one to whom we turned with our troubles, our questions, and our complaints. I remember my Liese deep in conversation with Hanni's Paula in her parents' apartment, or sitting on park benches, or helping us with our skates at the large football field that was transformed into an icerink in the winter.

Hanni was cuddly and round with dark curly hair, the very opposite from my ungainly, skinny figure with its straight fringe haircut. My mother's photograph of us squatting in the town park, staring into the camera, shows two very tidy and inquisitive small girls, but tells me nothing of our thoughts. When it was too cold or wet to play outside, we spent the afternoons in my or Hanni's room. I liked to visit her home. Her father and uncle owned a textile firm where they sold shimmering silks and other materials, and there was always the possibility that we might make an excursion into the stockrooms behind the shop. Hanni's mother's seductive Hungarian intonation also was a constant delight. Tante Boezsi, as I called her, knew how to turn their bolts of silk into exciting garments, a skill that later stood her in good stead. Hanni and I sat side by side throughout our years of elementary school and hid our secrets from our parents, the other children, and sometimes each other. On one occasion, we had a dreadful fight and refused to communicate for weeks. While I cannot remember the cause, I think of it as a cruelly unhappy period.

When not in school, we divided our time between Hanni's home and our apartment. My room, the *Kinderzim-*

mer, was furnished as a playroom, with my brass bed, a comfortable couch covered with a bearskin rug, a white table and chairs, a little desk, and numerous cupboards and shelves for my clothes, toys, and books.

My mother had the knack of understanding my greatest pleasures. The presentation of Christmas gifts took place on Christmas Eve in the dining room. A floor to ceiling tree decorated with small white candles, mingling their scent with the nostalgic aroma of pine needles, stood in the corner of the room. My parents and the maids prepared the tree. Every year, the doors were flung open so that my first view was of a glittering and shining tree with an array of gifts below. The nights when I first saw the small white oval table and chairs and my bedside lamp were the most enchanting Christmases I remember.

The small brass bedside lamp finally would make my reading in bed a legal delight for most of the time. Henceforth, I needed to read under the covers with my stolen flashlight only after the official good-night kisses had been exchanged. The table and chairs had been specially made by our local carpenter, Herr Hübner, to my mother's design. On another occasion, she had designed a swing, which he made for me. As both the outer and inner wall of this two-hundred-year-old house were extremely thick, all windows and doors were double, with wide, two- to three-foot spaces between them. One set of double doors led from my room to the dining room. The wooden swing was fastened in the space between them, and my friends and I used to hurl ourselves perilously from my room high over the dining room, barely avoiding the chandelier above the round mahogany table.

Sometime in my ninth year I was taught to crochet by Hilde Riedl, the needlework teacher at school, who happened to be the sister-in-law of my mother's friend Grete Moller. I became fascinated by this new game and had the brilliant idea of crocheting covers for the elegant brass door handles on all the sets of grand double doors in our apartment. For months I secretly crocheted these woolen sheaths, which looked rather like sausage skins in pale blue, pink, green, and purple. Finally I presented them nicely arranged in a shoebox as a Mother's Day gift to my deeply astonished mother. The poor woman then had to cover the beautiful old brass door handles throughout the apartment with my handiwork for a considerable time.

Another favorite sport was to settle in the broad windowsill of my room, where my friends and I made ourselves comfortable with large soft cushions. We had a view of the Herrengasse from the second floor and looked across at the forecourt of the Church of the Holy Ghost. The church was a treasure trove of entertainment. Our favorite happenings were weddings and funerals; christenings lagged somewhat behind. The weddings were all excitement and cheerfulness, with the romance of brides and bridesmaids, the guests in their finery arriving in cars or on foot. Funerals were equally intriguing, but somewhat nerve-wracking, as the corpse usually lay in state in the side chapel, which was also visible from my window.

Our maids, my friends, and I had well-organized signals so that we would not miss the processions and the high moments connected with the most impressive ecclesiastical events. Occasions like first communions or the Feast of the Assumption were special treats. On the latter day, large groups of children dressed in white gathered at the church and then walked in long procession, carrying baskets of roses from which they tossed petals on the streets between our church of the Holy Ghost and the parish church in the town center. Even on ordinary days, the church provided entertainment for our window-watching. Solitary worshipers ambled in throughout the day and lingered long enough to light a candle, make confession, and mumble a prayer.

These were enough to give hope to the old beggarwoman shrouded in black, who stood patiently outside the church. Occasionally we took her some bread or fruit. This ancient beggarwoman, a fixture in the right-hand corner by the church, stood for hours on the hard cobblestones. Her long black skirt hid the puddle she left behind her when she finally departed to whatever shelter she found after her day's vigil had ended.

The windowsill was interesting even when nothing much was happening at the church. We devised a game of lowering from the window onto the pavement below small items like papier-maché butterflies, cheap jewelry, or colored paper fastened to very fine threads. When unsuspecting pedestrians attempted to lift these we spirited them up into the air, and our giggles were rewarded with angry fists or cheerful smiles depending on the mood or character of the passerby.

Each one of the long and narrow baroque windows of the large expanse of government buildings to the right and left of the church opposite our house were splendidly candle-lit on special occasions, and particularly for the birthday of President Masaryk on the seventh of March. For most of my youth, I tried to convince my friends that these illuminations celebrated my father's birthday, as these two illustrious men shared the same day of birth.

The corner building next to our house was a little restaurant called the Inn of the Holy Ghost. The innkeeper's daughter, Liese, was another friend, and often came to share my window games. Truth to tell, however, I preferred to visit her at home, as her family lived in the kitchen of the inn, and when there I was able to watch the comings and goings of Liese's parents as they prepared the food and served it to their customers. Occasionally I would be offered a plate of pork, dumplings, and sauerkraut, tasting even better than that made by our cook Rosa.

My experiences with childhood friends were not always pleasurable. Once a week for a number of years, I brought home one of my orphaned classmates, Herta Mai, to share our midday meal. This arrangement was organized by the school and the orphanage. My mother had immediately volunteered to take part when the suggestion was made by our headmaster. Herta was a pale blonde with washed-out blue eyes. Together with my mother, she taught me a very important lesson. Her scholarly performance was not particularly distinguished, and one day, in the middle of eating our lentil soup, I began to brag about my own superior accomplishments. Feeling diminished, Herta began to cry and was unable to eat her soup. My mother was furious. She ordered me to fetch the dozen pretty new handkerchiefs that had a multicolored design of geometric dots somewhat like a Kandinsky painting. I adored these handkerchiefs, which I had received a few days earlier for my birthday. Mother then demanded that I make a present of the entire box to Herta and then bade her wipe her eyes and eat her soup. Now it was my turn to weep, and my parents had two sobbing children on their hands.

A constant companion during his stays in town was our landlord's nephew, Bubi Sobeck-Skal. Apart from the usual sessions in my windowsill, Bubi and I spent our time playing board games such as Halma, checkers, or chess, but we also enjoyed lurking in the garden and watching the various other tenants who wandered about the building. We were particularly interested in old Colonel Grabowski, a veteran of the First World War, who had a stiff leg, white muttonchop whiskers and mustaches, and limped about muttering curt acknowledgments to our overly polite greetings. The Grabowskis lived in two rooms next to our apartment on the middle floor of the Palais Sobeck-Skal, and we children were preoccupied with their domestic arrangements as they had no running water or built-in plumbing.

We discovered that their maid or the colonel collected buckets of water from the pump in the middle of the courtyard. At the same hour every day, with military precision, Colonel Grabowski, "der Herr Oberst," as we called him, wandered down to the lavatory in the courtyard right outside our cook's bedroom. We hid behind the courtyard pump, or behind the gooseberry hedge of the garden, in order to clock him in. Sometimes, if we had missed his appearance, we would run to inspect the lavatory and come out shrieking with laughter, announcing to each other that the unmistakable and lingering scent of his foul cigar confirmed his presence to the minute, as usual.

Bubi and I played rather more boisterous games than the make-believe games I played with my girlfriends. Apart from plaguing Colonel Grabowski, against my parents' expressed objections we often chased around the building, which was easy in a house of the size and design of the Palais Sobeck-Skal. There were two wonderful staircases. First, the main stairs, with wide, shallow, hardwood treads, that had been only slightly dented during their two-hundred-year existence. These stairs led from the porte cochere directly through the upper vestibule to our and the Grabowskis' front doors, and thence directly to the mansard floor. Opposite the main stairs in the porte cochere was the door to our kitchen, which adjoined the cook's bedroom. A second wooden spiral staircase lead straight up from the cook's bedroom past my bedroom door and further up into the attic that covered most of the mansard floor, where the washing was dried on wet winter days. The arrangement practically cried out for circular races through the house. We could run up the main stairs, through our apartment, up the spiral stairs into the attic, play hide and seek among the clotheslines full of wet or drying sheets, and then run down the spiral stairs into the kitchen, only to begin the whole circle again from the main stairs.

One evening during our breathless chase, the inevitable happened. While trying to prevent Bubi from catching me, my hand was trapped in the kitchen door, which Bubi smashed onto my right index finger. The pain of the squashed fingernail was excruciating, and my wails and cries of terror reverberated through the house. My parents, obviously, were not at home or this game would not have taken place. The cook called the doctor, who came immediately and ordered cold compresses and warned me that the nail would turn black and later fall off, and that the whole thing would be extremely painful during the foreseeable future. He was quite right, but forgot to mention that I would carry a scar from this episode to my dying day. My right index finger is twice the size of the other, and while the nail grew again, it has never been a normal shape. For the rest of the evening, Bubi was as white with fright as I was with pain and finally so unnerved that he kissed the back of my neck, a gesture totally unlike his usual undemonstrative self.

It was not Bubi, however, but two of my girlfriends who, without any appreciable success, tried to interest and instruct me in the mysteries of sex. The first was Ruth, about a year older than I.

Ruth and her family lived in a large house with a splendid garden on the outskirts of our town. My mother and I had been bidden to tea on a lovely summer afternoon. After we had eaten, our mothers settled down to a nice gossip, and we girls were sent to amuse ourselves in the garden. Ruth beckoned me to follow her down the slope into the greenery. I stumbled after her through a water garden and a rockery while she pointed out all her father's favorite plants, though I was unable to appreciate any of his prize-winning beauties. Finally we reached a small pavilion at the far end of the garden.

Inside, this little hut was comfortably furnished with a couch and chairs, a place obviously much used for reading and other quiet activities. Ruth immediately settled down on a wicker chair and told me to sit on the couch opposite. She was usually preoccupied with her music, her books, or her study of birds, which she had begun very young, having been inspired by the large aviary in the town park. She bent toward me in what I expected to be a serious conversation. "Take your panties off," she commanded.

I was not unreasonably startled and hesitated. "Come on, we don't have all day," she scolded briskly. What Ruth was after was a close inspection of my secret anatomy. She got down on her knees, lifted my skirt, and, having satisfied her curiosity by pulling and prodding me about, offered herself for my inspection. Well prepared in advance, she had come down to the garden without her panties. In fact, I disappointed her deeply, as I was far too bashful to look at the interesting research material she presented and kept my eyes firmly shut.

Another friend was equally unsuccessful with my sexual instruction, though she did manage to raise my erotic consciousness. Ilse, who attended my school, was the daughter of a concierge on the other side of town. Her father was the carpenter, Herr Hübner, who often built intricate pieces of furniture for my parents according to my mother's design.

Ilse and I became great friends. Occasionally she came to play in my house, but I often went to see her, finding it fascinating to watch her father at work and to imagine where the tables, chairs, or bookshelves that emerged from his clever hands would find homes. As her mother was the concierge, it was also fun to be in their room and hear her mother deal with the tenants' complaints regarding problems in the building.

Early on, Ilse and I began the wonderful game of

inventing and acting out stories. We imagined ourselves to be many different people, including our own parents or their friends, the teachers in our school, shopkeepers in the town, the tenants in Ilse's building, or characters in fiction. When we had exhausted known characters, we made them up. Then we invented situations and happenings in their lives that were a mixture of reality as we knew it from the world around us, the books we read, the films or plays we heard people talk about, and again out of our imagination. We worked up stories dealing with business, school, or family problems, but also romantic kitsch about courtship and disaster both for people we could reconstruct and for fairytale figures such as princes and princesses. It was a game without end, and we never tired of it. We could spin out these stories over days, or even weeks, waiting eagerly for school to be over so that we might be alone to continue our play. On the whole, the plots we devised dealt with the realities we knew about, whether from our own observation or what we understood from fiction. The unimaginable and unexperienced were not in our purview.

One day, however, Ilse announced that we must include what happens after the kiss with which all movies seemed to end. She insisted that she knew what this must be. Since her family all shared a single bedroom, she had seen her parents do it. I could not imagine what she was talking about, but agreed to go along with the procedure. So we no longer ended romantic stories with a chaste final curtain kiss. Instead we tumbled, fully dressed, to the floor and rolled about in each other's arms moaning and groaning with all our might and, usually, giggling helplessly. After a while, this performance became the standard ending to the romantic part of our stories.

All went well until a certain afternoon, when absorbed in our pseudo-copulation we did not notice Bertha, our cook, who came silently into my playroom and stood transfixed watching our antics. She asked what we were doing, and when we explained that we were "making love," she commanded us to stop immediately. She went on to condemn this game as totally unacceptable and threatened to tell my mother what we had been doing, unless we agreed to certain conditions that she would explain to us later. Her attitude was so unpleasant that we agreed, fearing that my mother's reaction might be even worse.

Bertha's conditions when finally laid down to us were the following. She wanted us to accompany her to her boyfriend's home and there to repeat our performance in his presence. I didn't feel very happy about this, but the thought of my mother's wrath forced me to persuade Ilse that we should comply with Bertha's demands. The performance duly took place at the boyfriend's rooms. Our audience consisted of Bertha and her friend Karl convulsed with laughter, while Ilse and I rolled about the floor groaning and moaning rather halfheartedly. When we had done our party piece, we were given some hot chocolate and cake. Bertha then walked us home, one on each side demurely holding her hands. To all appearances we were two innocent little girls out for a walk with their nanny.

The episode left me with a feeling of unease and spoiled the pleasure we had taken in our games. I was just as ignorant as I had been before about the mystery of sex. But I now felt that there was something strangely unpleasant about it, perhaps funny, but certainly secret, and not to be talked about.

It was quite some years later that Joe, two years older than I, the son of my mother's friend Hebs, tried to improve my academic sexual instruction. Hebs Weisshuhn was one of my mother's more romantic friends. As I did most of my mother's friends, I called her Aunt or "Tante." Tante Hebs originally came from Riga and spoke with a marshmallow Baltic accent that produced little frissons of delight. She was blue-eyed with soft blond curls and had a face like a warm, round cat. She had been married and divorced before we knew her, and Joe was her son from her first marriage. She was introduced to my parents by her second husband, Charlie Weisshuhn, the owner of a wooded estate with a sawmill and paper factory in the nearby village of Žimrovice. The woods and forests of Czechoslovakia were a staple for the production of paper, and the Weisshuhns moved between Vienna and the Czech forests that were cut and turned into paper or furniture.

Tante Hebs visited us frequently. She also traveled much, even to England where she had old friends, and she always came back with interesting clothes and presents for my mother and me. I remember her returning from London and bringing a splendid full-length, glazed chintz dressing-gown with large multicolored flowers on a black ground, which my mother wore for many years and which rustled excitingly whenever she moved. Both my mother and I were sad when this garment had to be retired.

Hebs and Charlie Weisshuhn lived in a spacious villa in the woods surrounding their sawmill, and my mother and I sometimes spent some days with them during the summer. In the country Hebs looked quite different, as she wore a scarf around her head, showing almost no hair to protect it from the sawdust. I always loved being near Tante Hebs, but being with them in the country was the best, because of Joe. Joe's extra two years, not to mention the absence of his father, gave him a real cachet. He was fair-haired like his mother and had an accent that, though less compelling than hers, was different enough from those I knew to be exciting. Not that Joe took a great deal of notice of me at first. A girl, and one as young as I, was hardly a fit companion. He had his own friends among the village boys and was usually off somewhere in the woods, appearing only for meals and sometimes not even then.

I spent most of my time in Žimrovice roaming around the woods, paddling in the stream, and playing the usual word and board games with my mother and Tante Hebs. They also taught me a Double Patience at which I soon became expert. (As old ladies in their seventies, Tante Hebs and my mother were still playing their Double Patience in England.)

Gradually, during my visits to Žimrovice, Joe allowed me to accompany him on his excursions into the woods. We went to gather berries or wild mushrooms. There were wonderful wild strawberries in the early summer and masses of shrubs bearing luscious small blueberries later. We filled large red enameled cooking pots, intoxicated by their scent as we carried them back to the house in the hot summer sunshine. Those blueberries tasted delicious raw, but even better cooked and enveloped in huge yeast dumplings, eaten hot with sugar and melted butter. Sometimes my mother and I took large jugs of them back to town, which our cook Rosa made into mouthwatering *Streuselkuchen*. As it sat cooling on the shelves circling the larder, its aroma wafted tantalizingly through the whole house.

After a while, Joe decided that I was reasonably trustworthy and suggested that we leave the blueberry woods and explore the woodstacks instead. These were carefully arranged closer to the sawmill in preparation for the next stage of their transformation into paper. We clambered about on the woodstacks, sitting on top of them, eating handfuls of blueberries and occasionally some sandwiches we had brought from the house. One late afternoon Joe suggested I come out to play on the woodstacks, and we wandered off towards the sawmill. On the way over, he made me promise never, ever to tell anyone about what he was about to show me. I promised fervently, and he led me to a stack we had often sat upon, somewhat separate from the rest. There he removed a log from a side wall of the stack, and, to my surprise, this produced an opening large enough for us to crawl through. The inside was quite hollow and primitively furnished with a table and stools created from small logs. A low candle was burning in a glass container, and when I was accustomed to the darkness, I became aware that we were not alone, but that three older boys roughly of Joe's age were sitting around the little cave.

Joe introduced me as his friend, and they mumbled some unenthusiastic greeting. It appeared that they were engaged in a game of cards, and Joe quickly joined in, telling me to watch carefully so that I might learn it. They played for a while until I had mastered the idea, and then I was able to take part. This game, the Black Cat, became an evocative and mysterious part of my education.

After we had played a few rounds, and the boys had accepted my presence, they came to the next stage in what appeared to be a ritual in this woodstack. The boy with the deepest voice fumbled about in his pockets and pulled out a small tin of cigarettes. I realized that this was the high point of their gathering. A cigarette was lit from the candle and passed around the group. Everyone solemnly took a puff, and when all the boys had had their turn, they politely offered it to me. I was overcome by the mystery, the secrecy, and the honor bestowed upon me, a girl, and a little girl, much younger than the boys in the group. I hoped I would acquit myself well, but I had never smoked before and was dreadfully afraid of coughing or choking or, even worse, being sick. I took a tiny puff and was relieved to find that, though the taste was pretty foul, nothing drastic happened. The cigarette went around to all, myself included, until it was finished. I was tremendously excited at having managed to smoke without mishap, elated and proud to be accepted by the group. We played a few more rounds of the Black Cat, and then Joe and I ran back to the house for supper.

Tante Hebs and my mother were busy with their own affairs and didn't notice that Joe and I had a new bond, our secret now creating a shared intimacy between us. It was many years before I realized just how scandalously naughty we had been to smoke inside a stack of wood, surrounded by drying logs as far as the eye could see. No wonder Joe had sworn me to secrecy.

Joe went to a different elementary school from mine, but when, aged eleven, I entered the Gymnasium he was already there, in a higher class, and we saw each other occasionally. By this time, thanks to my being able to keep a secret, Joe continued to initiate me into the adult world. This took the form of looking up risqué words in the dictionary. Every so often he would pass me a slip of paper as we met on the stairs, in the corridor, or during morning break, when the whole school paraded around the street in front of the building. These slips of paper gave me the page numbers of the dictionary, and the words to be learned in our special code, so that no one else could read them. This intricate method of education worked only up to a point. When handed on in this manner, words like *vagina*, *menses*, or *copulation* sound intriguing, even daring, but the dictionary explanation is innocuous and insufficient to clarify the mysteries of sex.

My mother began to wonder why I was suddenly so taken with the study of words. I would wait until she had left the house and I could spend some time alone with the large dictionary in the glass-covered bookcase in the living room to decipher Joe's code. The process would take a while as each word could lead to several others before I decided that the explanations were inadequate for one of my limited experience. It would never do to admit this to Joe, and in any case it would have been far too embarrassing to discuss our enigmatic words in person. So he continued to pass me his coded slips of paper, and the excitement of receiving them was a satisfying end in itself for the time being. And, of course, the idea of sharing these incomprehensible matters with the fourteen-year-old Joe gave the situation a wonderful aura of romance.

It must have been sometime before Joe began to instruct me in this manner that I came upon a letter written by my mother to some friends living in Germany in which she expressed her admiration for their courage in deciding to bring a child into the world at this moment. These friends were on the point of emigrating to Australia, and I was fascinated by the fact that my mother should write to them so openly about a subject she had never discussed with me, or with anyone else in my hearing. I clearly remember the letter lying on the sewing-machine table, where I suppose she had left it while discussing some domestic sewing matter with the woman who came to mend the linen and sew some of my clothes. Of course I was curious as to why this was not the proper moment to have children, but since I felt guilty having read a private letter and, moreover, the subject was clearly taboo I did not dare to ask.

Not only my mother's friends, the pretend aunts, like Joe's mother, Tante Hebs, but at least one real aunt was an important part of my world. My father had four sisters: Anna, Ida, Emmy, and Valli. Tante Anna was my godmother, but she died soon after I was born. Tante Ida lived in Slovakia, where she was married to a lawyer, and I only met her once, when I stayed with her over Easter. (She perished as she tried to escape the Nazis by tramping over the Carpathian mountains with her grandson.) Tante Emmy came to stay with us once a year and always brought me chocolates, which I treasured and saved for as long as I could, eating only one each day. I never discovered what happened to Tante Emmy. Tante Valli was sent to Auschwitz.

Valli, the youngest of my father's sisters, is the only

one I really knew, as she lived not too far from us in the town of Jägerndorf. She was married to a doctor and had two sons, Max and Ernst. By the time I remember her, she was a widow, and her sons, quite grown up, lived elsewhere, probably in Vienna or possibly in Prague. People said I resembled Tante Valli, which I liked to hear, as they also said that she was pretty, in fact the most beautiful of my father's sisters. She was very gentle and knew how to make me feel at home, although she carried an air of melancholy.

Jägerndorf was a town somewhat smaller than Troppau, and not particularly interesting, but I was taken there to see Tante Valli's special oculist as my eyes began to give trouble early on in my school career. He prescribed glasses for reading the blackboard, and after this life in the classroom was easier. Occasionally I was sent to stay with Tante Valli to keep her company. I always understood that my parents thought it would be especially good for me to visit Tante Valli, though it took me quite a long time to discover exactly why this should be.

I enjoyed going there, as Tante Valli made sure my visit was a success. She invited other children to play with me and sent her maid to take me shopping and occasionally to the park. Sometimes Tante Valli arranged for Karl, the son of one of her friends, to take me to the municipal swimming pool. As he was at least three years older than I, this was always quite thrilling, but also unnerving. I found it difficult to make conversation with Karl, but he didn't seem to notice. He helped my swimming lessons considerably, as I was ashamed to let him know how frightened I was of the water, and on my return to Troppau, my mother was delighted to find that I was able to move about the deep end of the pool quite happily without the safety ring to which I had clung during the previous season.

My mother's uncle, my Great-uncle Sigi, also lived in

Jägerndorf, and occasionally, when I was out walking, I met him coming along the street. Each time this happened, he stopped to greet me and pulled a nasty sticky sweet out of the pocket of his coat. I always thanked him as politely as I could, despite the fact that the sweets were invariably coated with fluff from his pockets, where they must have languished for months. One time Karl, accompanying me, was also offered a sweet and choked when he put it into his mouth. I had to explain that I put up with these sweets because I didn't know how to tell Uncle Sigi that they were inedible, and I was relieved to find that Karl did not know how to deal with Uncle Sigi any better than I.

Tante Valli's maid used to cook a delicious dish that we never had at home, but which I later found to be a favorite English breakfast: bacon and eggs. I loved this dish and begged our cook Rosa to copy it when I returned. Of course, it was never really like the English dish, because the bacon was quite different, and it was put on fried rye bread with caraway seeds, which would never happen in England. However, the fried bread and pork covered with eggs remains a special Jägerndorf memory.

Tante Valli told me wonderful stories that she made up as she went along. Sometimes she came out walking with me, with her cane, but more often she stayed at home playing the piano. She was a superb pianist, and my parents told me that years before she had wanted to become a professional. As so often, marriage and children had intervened, and then her sight began to fade, but Tante Valli continued to play, especially after her husband had died. She often played for me, and I loved listening to her and spent many evenings comfortably in her darkening room while she practiced from memory for hours.

One evening we sat thus, I on the sofa listening, and Tante Valli playing, when a violent storm erupted with great bursts of thunder and lightning. I was very frightened of the lightning, quite sure that it would strike directly into our house, and suggested that we should hide in the cupboard. But Tante Valli continued to play quite calmly and told me to shut my eyes, so that I would not see the lightning. "As you see," she said, "it does not trouble me at all." Tante Valli was blind.

CHAPTER
3

SOME TIME AFTER THIS occasion, on a wintry December morning of 1937, my parents announced that I was going to visit my mother's friend Tante Resl in Olmütz. My mother and Tante Resl had been childhood friends, since their fathers had known each other from their Viennese student days. Olmütz, or Olomouc in Czech, was about forty miles southwest of Troppau, and the two families had retained close ties. It was, as I have said, the Klimt portrait of Madame Primavesi of Olmütz that had so vividly reminded me of my childhood experiences. As soon as I saw his portrait of Eugenia Primavesi, I was poignantly reminded of Tante Resl Sonnenschein. She had a very round face, with prominent thyroidal eyes, and a plump figure, usually draped (even as late as the 1930s) in flowing Klimtian garments.

Resl Sonnenschein never married. In her thirties, she frequently stayed with us in Troppau. My mother and I used to look forward to Tante Resl's biannual visits. As she had often visited my grandparents since childhood, she knew the town well and had many friends in common with my mother. She was also expected to entertain me. She always came with two large suitcases full of exquisite lingerie, which she had designed and sewn herself and then sold to her friends during her visit. I remember my delight, when, aged nine or ten, I received a light, spring-green chemise covered with tiny pink rosebuds, made especially for me.

As soon as Tante Resl arrived, my parents invited all their bachelor friends. A particular favorite was the ascetic Franz-Joseph Häusler, who lived in mysterious somber rooms in a medieval house belonging to the ancient Order of St. John. There, attended by his equally somber manservant, he filled his time researching family trees and executing them on large sheets of parchment for the minor aristocracy. In retrospect, a less likely companion for Tante Resl is hard to imagine. At the time I judged all these friends of my parents quite simply as suitable or unsuitable companions for myself. And indeed, both Tante Resl and Franz-Joseph Häusler passed that test with flying colors.

When my parents told me I was going to stay with Tante Resl in Olmütz, they presented me with a brand-new black lacquer and pigskin suitcase of my very own. I and my suitcase were put on the train; Tante Resl and her father collected me from the Olmütz station. Of course, Tante Resl, being single, lived with her parents. I found their dark, silent apartment in the center of the town rather oppressive, in contrast to our own home, which was so light and airy, overlooking as it did a garden on one side and a wide open street with its intriguing church on the other.

Not only the apartment but also the dinner table conversation of the Sonnenscheins was somewhat oppressive. Try as they would they seemed unable not to speak of politics. They were right to be concerned, of course, since this was the winter in which Hitler was beginning to make his assault on Austria and the Austrian Chancellor Schuschnigg had several dismal discussions with him, which ended with Austria's *Anschluss* (or connection) to Germany and Hitler's triumphant entry into Vienna in March of 1938. But despite these worries, the Sonnenscheins did their best to entertain me. Tante Resl's mother tempted me with delicious dishes like plum dumplings with cinnamon and sugar; her doctor father showed me the skeleton in his consulting room at the end of their apartment; and Tante Resl herself took me for walks in the town. We pelted each other with snowballs in the park and admired the famous fifteenth-century astronomical clock near the town hall. We ignored, either because of Tante Resl's ignorance, or because of her empathy with my tender age, the internationally renowned medieval manuscripts in the archbishop's library. Best of all, we spent much time in a splendid *Konditorei*, having pastries and hot chocolate, which contributed to Tante Resl's delightfully plump figure.

One day Tante Resl and I visited a family whom I had met during a summer vacation at a country spa, whose daughter was my age. She had the same name, the same coloring, and the same fringe haircut as I. Her mother brought out some snapshots taken that summer of the two of us, lying face down and stretched out on the grass. We were clad in nothing but our panties, our flat-chested childish bodies exposed to the world. I was asked to determine who was who. (I still have my copy of this photograph.) I remember my astonishment on that occasion, when I looked at the differences in our bodies, even though we were the same age. The other Suse was considerably rounder and more muscular, my buttocks almost flat in comparison, and my waist and shoulders so slight. I considered my mother and Tante Resl and thought about the difference in their bodies. My mother tall and slim, Tante Resl short and pudgy. How different would my friend and I be, once we were grown, I wondered. Alas, I never found out. From this afternoon tea party, we returned to the Sonnenschein apartment and serious grown-up conversation immediately took place behind the closed consulting room door. Tante Resl eventually emerged, a sad expression on her kind round face, and told me that my parents had telephoned and wanted us to call back. The news, which, for some inexplicable reason, will forever be connected in my mind with my black suitcase, rather than any other parts of the Olmütz visit, was that my grandfather had died. I had, in fact, been sent away because they knew he was dying, and, as usual, my parents had wanted to spare me the grimmer realities of life. His last words, my mother told me, were, "We are all children of God." The allusion escaped me. I puzzled about this for a long time. What did he mean? I wondered. And how could my grandfather think of himself as a child?

The Sonnenscheins and I began to talk about my grandparents. I told them of my weekly luncheons with my grandfather, which I both enjoyed and dreaded. Every Friday, since I had been about six, I had had my midday meal with my grandfather. Meanwhile our cook and maids cleaned our house, and my parents were at their large reserved table at the Weinstube Morgenstern on the Niederring, where any of their friends could join them.

For these Friday luncheons I was escorted to the rather sad apartment into which Grandfather had moved after my grandmother died. As at home, I was expected to eat everything whether I liked it or not. But Grandfather's cook produced food far less delicious than our fare at home. Occasionally, during the meal, Grandfather removed his teeth. I never quite understood why and did not dare to ask. But I used to wait for this maneuver expectantly and was both intrigued and repulsed by it. At the end of the meal, he let me pull a long thin straw from the center of his cigar, which he then lit very deliberately. After he had smoked it, he would play Brahms or Beethoven on the piano with controlled passion, while I, quietly bored, sat waiting to be collected by my nursemaid and taken home. Very occasionally, my Uncle Fritz, who had studied law in Prague, would be there either with or without his latest lady friend, and that was the best time of all. Uncle Fritz was warm and funny. He told nice stories, sat me on his lap, and was interested in my small problems and triumphs. When Uncle Fritz came with his lady friends, Grandfather was more austere than ever. Sometimes he played chess with Uncle Fritz, while the lady friend and I waited restlessly for one or the other of them to shout, "Checkmate!"

Tante Resl explained that my parents wanted me to stay with her until after Grandfather's funeral. I stayed another couple of days, and she then accompanied me back to Troppau. She remained for a few weeks, a support for my mother and a good companion for me. There was a grand sorting out of my grandfather's things, of which I remember nothing, except that my father stored all kinds of mysterious Jewish artifacts in a beautiful antique cupboard in our vestibule. There they remained until the Gestapo search in October of 1938 discovered them. I remember my parents saying to each other, and to many others, how glad they were that my grandfather had died when he did and had thus been spared "the horror."

Unfortunately Tante Resl was not spared the horror. On a gray afternoon in London, after the end of the war in 1945, my mother told me that Resl had volunteered to take charge of a Jewish children's transport bound for Switzerland. The transport had been diverted to Auschwitz.

That spring, after my visit to Olmütz and my grandfather's death, the whole Sudeten German problem became a major political and diplomatic crisis in Europe. At the Versailles Treaty after the First World War, the governments of France and Great Britain had guaranteed Czechoslovakia's frontiers. Now Hitler and his henchman, the Sudeten leader Konrad Henlein, were beginning to force the hand of the Czech government, which made it almost obligatory for France and Great Britain to intervene. Henlein presented a speech in Karlsbad at the end of April 1938 in which he demanded specific boundaries for German-speaking territories in Czechoslovakia as separate from the rest of the Czech state; he also demanded legal concessions and German-speaking, instead of Czech, officials for all German territories and their public right to proclaim their allegiance to the ideology of the Third Reich. Having watched Hitler swallow up Austria in March of that year, the world waited anxiously to see what would happen in the Sudetenland. British, French, and Hitler's German envoys had numerous discussions, and the Czech government in Prague prepared for elections to discover the will of its population. Toward the end of May the whole of Europe believed that the German army was massed on the Czech borders ready to invade. And by May 21 the Czechs had quickly prepared a strong line of defense, consisting of its standing army and thousands of enthusiastic volunteers. The Czechs having thus called Hitler's bluff, the German army did not invade at this time, and the world breathed a small sigh of relief— but not for long.

My knowledge of this political background was nonexistent at the time. However, I have a vivid memory of my parents, and several of their friends including Grete Moller and myself, setting off in our old black "Praga" motorcar on May 21. We drove to an interior village in order to escape the possible battle as our homes were so close to the border. For two nights, while the Czech army was entrenched along the border, we stayed in a small hotel.

There we existed with a strict blackout, and the grownups listened to the radio and had endless and, to me, incomprehensible discussions, while members of the group took it in turn to amuse me with card and other games. I assume they thought me too fragile to burden with the problems and fears that were uppermost in their minds. But in retrospect I wonder whether my future life would not have been quite different if they had tried to explain the situation to me and allowed me to comprehend and come to terms with the world in which we lived.

Apart from Tante Resl, my mother's oldest and closest friend was Grete Moller. Their mothers, also, had been friends, and they had been pushed side by side in their baby carriages through the town of Troppau, in which both they and I had been born. Later they had been in school together, and I have their class photograph showing them as small girls: my mother taller, more sophisticated, her expression dark and somber, while Grete's round, dimpled face had the delightfully innocent sparkle that she retained into her eighties.

Tante Grete was a constant presence not only in my childhood but throughout my life until she died. She told me that she saw my father jump onto a tram on his way to the clinic, shouting to her, "It's a girl," on the day when I was born. When visiting my grandparents, I would often meet her walking arm-in-arm with her father, a bearded figure reminiscent of Freud, whose helplessly shaking hands made me feel so uncomfortable.

Grete was divorced from her husband, a journalist on the *Prager Tagblatt*. Although this husband, Bruno, was a charming and witty man, he was an alcoholic and had made her life intolerable. This, of course, I discovered only much, much later. When I was a child, Bruno was a mysterious name, and Grete usually appeared in the company of a handsome actor called Leo. In her youth, she was the only one of my mother's girlhood friends who attended a university. She studied chemistry and pharmacology at the Charles University in Prague and then after her divorce returned to Troppau and opened the Drogerie Moller, the pharmacy of my childhood dreams.

The Drogerie Moller was located in the center of town, first in a rather long narrow shop, and later in a bright and modern new building that Grete owned jointly with a woman friend. For me, both places resembled jewel caskets. Every day at noon and again in the early evening, my father and mother met there when he came from his office, and they then went home together to eat. Before I was old enough to go to school, and later, during the vacations, I always accompanied my mother to this rendezvous.

While we waited for my father, Tante Grete and my mother gossiped and I was given free rein of the shop and its tantalizing stock. The medical part, the pharmacy, where she prepared pills and potions, was, of course, out of bounds, but the cosmetics and toilet articles were a cornucopia of treasure. I loved the soaps, the pretty bottles of perfume, the lipsticks, combs, and small cosmetic bags. There were also tiny samples of everything that seemed made to order just for me. My greatest delight was to be able to sell some of Grete's stock to strangers. But in the absence of real customers, I plagued my mother until she bought various unnecessary delights from Grete's shelves. I suppose most of the things I "sold" were surreptitiously returned when I was not there.

Tante Grete's new Drogerie was part of the complex containing the ancient Schmetterhaus, the central feature of our town. This building, with an easily recognizable imposing tower and a roof of brightly colored, shimmering tiles, incorporated several shops and restaurants. The most important of these landmarks, the well-known Café Niedermeyer, overlooked the Oberring (the upper ring), where street markets used to set up in the Middle Ages. By now this market had been moved to the Niederring (the lower ring), and the Oberring was merely a large open space between the Schmetterhaus and the town theater, the latter a quite splendid building of classical proportions.

The theater was one of the beneficiaries of the town's having been the capital city of Silesia during the empire and of the cultural connections and interests of the Viennese civil servants who retired here. It offered first-rate repertory companies, plays, and operas that had been, or were about to be, performed in Vienna. My first visit to this building was to hear Humperdinck's opera *Hansl and Gretl*; both the music and the anticipation of the nastiness of the witch are still clearly in my memory. On one occasion I was asked to write a review of a children's ballet, *Die Puppenfee*, for Fritz Troester, a friend of my parents, who was the theater critic for the local newspaper. Of this I remember nothing but Troester's quizzical expression when I complained that the chief character, the Doll Fairy, had abnormally fat legs and could not therefore be a genuine fairy. Tante Grete's admirer, Leo, acted both in Vienna and in our local theater. Her sister, Herta, had a friend whom she married years later and who was the basso in the Vienna opera and sang frequently in the theater in Troppau.

Herta herself conducted a dance and gymnastic studio that I attended from a very early age. I enjoyed myself hugely choreographing solitary ballets that I practiced for hours accompanied by the radio in our drawing room. But both my debut and my final curtain as a ballerina took place in Herta's studio amidst great audience enthusiasm. Compared to her sister, Grete, Herta seemed rather severe, but then I didn't appreciate her wry sense of humor until I was properly grown up. She also had a great sense of elegance. In the days when I played at being a salesgirl in Grete's shop, Herta, on her way to meet her opera singer, Robert, once gave me a memorable thrill. From the most mysterious of the shop's drawers, she slipped into her handbag one of the little packets joked about by the boys in our cook's village. I did not comprehend in the least what these were, or indeed their purpose. I understood only that this was something to do with grownup behavior and therefore not quite nice.

In October 1938, when I was dismissed from school and began my English lessons with Tante Elsa, I overheard my mother tell my father in a still small voice: "Grete has been taken prisoner." I could not imagine this. Tante Grete was practically a member of the family. She always came to our Christmas celebrations, to my birthday parties, and often dined with us or with my parents at their reserved tables in the town hostelries. Sometimes we spent vacations together in hotels in the mountains. She was the kindest, most reliable, and most amusing of my "aunts." How could she be in prison? What had she done?

Many years later after Grete's death, her real niece, Joanna, showed me a short piece that Grete had written about this terrifying period of her life. Two Gestapo men had come for her at seven o'clock in the evening, just as she was about to lock up her shop. They screamed obscenities at her—"Jewish Devils," "Pigshit," "Pigsty," "Enough already." In her short essay Grete described the shock that almost made her faint, the terrified faces of her trusted old employees. Then the helplessness of having her handbag taken from her and being pushed into a cell with ten wooden bunks. Only one woman was in this cell when she arrived; by the end of her stay she was sharing it with twelve others. The worst of this period was not the indignity, although this too she described with great pathos; it was the uncertainty, not knowing what would happen next, whether one would ever come out of this situation alive.

These women began to know and accept each other despite their often unbridgeable differences. They were of all classes, Jews, socialists, communists, all types of "undesirables" of the Third Reich.

Grete was very graphic in her assessment of the differences in attitude between the women prisoners and the men. She describes how the women enjoyed their very infrequent communal baths. How, at first, they were ashamed of their nakedness, but gradually began to take a delight in the beauty of their bodies. How they enjoyed the fresh air and sunshine during the endless perambulation they were expected to make in the courtyard. They sang, and even danced, in order to comfort themselves. Years later, in England, she met one of the men who had been imprisoned on the floor above. He told her how enviously they used to watch the women enjoying their open-air period from their windows. She also remembers how occasionally the women stood on their bunks and watched the men, many of whom were familiar figures, in the courtyard (something they had been strictly forbidden to do). They were horrified at the deterioration, the unshaven faces, the shambling hopelessness of the men's gait. It was an interesting comparison. She was puzzled but could find no good reason for the differences. Perhaps, she thought, men were more used to being in charge of themselves and thus found it harder to be forced to give up their autonomy.

I knew none of this at the time. When, after six weeks, she was released and told to leave the country immediately, Tante Grete came straight to our house. After being allowed to greet her, I was quickly sent to bed. It was a sad and frightening evening. Through the slightly open doors, I heard the somber voices of a conversation that went on for hours. So far the Gestapo had not come near us, but my parents were obviously afraid of what might happen next. When both my mother and Tante Grete were in their eighties, I had the chilling experience of arriving in my mother's empty London flat from San Francisco on my birthday. My mother had collapsed and been taken into Westminster Hospital the day before. Waiting for me on the dining table, I found a bouquet of roses and a small bottle of perfume brought by special messenger. Although crippled, and unable to traverse London, Tante Grete, reliable as always, had remembered the day when I was born and, as if we were both still in Troppau, had sent me something from the Drogerie Moller.

By the time of Tante Grete's frightening experience in the local jail in 1938, our domestic staff had shrunk to one maid-of-all-work. This was Martha, a young woman from a nearby village, who was a devoted Seventh-Day Adventist. Martha had begun work in our household as a parlormaid several years earlier. At that time we still had the cook Rosa, the nursemaid Liese, the chauffeur Edwin, and the charwoman Frau Emma (a kind woman, whose many children occasionally kept me company, and whom I remember chiefly for the fact that she used to clean our Persian carpets with sauerkraut), all of whom had been with us ever since I could remember. By 1938 all of them had left, except Martha. I did not really know Martha as well as I had most of the other servants, because she had not been with us very long, and being the only one, she was far too busy. They, on the other hand, had had specific duties and more time to bother with me. Nevertheless, Martha is more a part of our family in my memory than any of the others because of the unusual services she performed for us, services that were certainly over and above what one might expect of a maid.

It was not only our domestic staff that had shrunk by 1938; our living accommodation also had changed drastically. My father had closed the offices in which, for many years, he had conducted his law practice in the town center. In their place my parents' bedroom and my mother's beautiful sunny salon had been converted into professional legal offices. My parents' expressions had changed from relaxed imperturbability to unsmiling masks. My father no longer spent his usual three hours during the middle of the day in the local café playing chess, bridge, or billiards. My mother had given up her shopping expeditions, not to speak of her visits to the opera or the theater or even to her friends. The streets were noisy with singing and marching, and radio announcements about troop movements in Austria seemed to have a riveting fascination for my parents and their friends.

As I was now twelve years old, I should, of course, have been attending the secondary school, the humanistic Gymnasium to which I had been admitted, diligently. And indeed, I had started the first year, delighted to be addressed formally by my family name rather than my first name as had been the practice at the elementary school. Moreover, in contrast to the girls' elementary school, here we were all in one classroom, boys and girls together, although we sat on opposite sides of a central aisle. Furthermore, we were now being taught by a variety of teachers, each dealing with only one subject, rather than a general teacher for each grade. Having numerous teachers was much more interesting. Their characters often seemed to suit the subject of their discussion, and even more intriguing was the fact that my mother remembered some of them from her own schooldays. This seemed to be a common generational experience in our small provincial town. My mother and her friends vied with each other in telling wonderful stories about the teachers in whose classrooms I now found myself, and they boasted about how much better, worse, or peculiar these men and women had been a generation earlier.

By this time I was old enough to walk through the

town park alone and able to dawdle as much as I pleased on the way to and from school. The walk through the park was one I knew intimately. My father was an early riser, and I had spent many happy spring and summer mornings trying to keep up with his long strides during our walks before breakfast, while my mother was still asleep. I also used to walk through another part of the park to my weekly French lessons at the apartment of my mother's old friend Joanna. I have to thank her for my pronunciation of this language, which even many further years of Anglicized instruction of French could not dislodge. The end of the central avenue traversing the park opened up to the humanistic Gymnasium, a large building of elegant classical proportions. Every day, during the morning break, the entire student body circled around the pavement in front of the school, with a small group of teachers, like warders, keeping a sharp eye on us from the middle of the circle.

One morning in October 1938, as I arrived rather breathlessly in my classroom, I was told to present myself in the principal's office immediately. I could not imagine what scrape I had got myself into, but ran up the wide staircase and found two older students, also waiting nervously in front of the headmaster's door. We were ushered in and invited to sit down in front of his imposing desk. To my utter bewilderment, this large red-faced man, unable to meet our eyes, told us between many lengthy pauses and clearings of the throat that it would be advisable for the three of us not to come back to school until further notice. The other two seemed to understand what this was all about. I was completely baffled, but far too intimidated to ask any questions of the headmaster or of my fellow pupils.

I went back to my classroom, collected my satchel and books, and started down the steps at the front of the building. The school was parading in the usual circle around the pavement, and as I and the two others who had been in the headmaster's study crossed the circle, a menacing grumbling suddenly erupted into a long drawn-out howl. I became frightened and, starting to run, soon found myself pursued by some of the larger boys from the senior class. They shouted something that I didn't understand and then seemed to lose interest and returned to the parade. The teacher-warders, clustered in the center of the circle, had not moved.

When I returned home in tears, my parents were finally forced to explain what was happening. The Nazis had taken over the Sudetenland. Jews were undesirable in this new state. Although we were not religiously affiliated Jews, all four of my grandparents had been Jewish, and by Hitler's laws we were therefore part of this group. We would have to find a way of leaving the country, probably move to America or Great Britain, and to this end I should soon be learning to speak English. I puzzled about the word *undesirable*. What did it really mean? And who exactly thought me undesirable? If my school friends thought me undesirable, why had they always been happy to be with me? It didn't make sense.

While this was surely the most disturbing crisis of my young life, my parents' calm explanation soothed the pain and prevented me from panicking about the future. Even more important, they knew how much I had enjoyed school and quickly organized another absorbing occupation for me.

The next day I began my English lessons. This meant going to the house of my English-speaking "Aunt" Elsa, who lived at the other end of town, about three times farther away from our home than my school. I had to walk through the town park in the opposite direction from the Gymnasium. On the first day, Martha accompanied me to Aunt Elsa's, but I returned alone after the lesson. I had not told my parents about the unpleasant behavior of the older

boys at school, and as they seemed to think it safe for me
to walk through the park to Aunt Elsa's for the next three
months, I saw no reason to burden them with any misgivings. Although I never managed to complete this walk without a feeling of unease and sometimes dread, only once was
I plagued by further harassment, when a group of boys
from my school chased up from behind and pelted me with
stones. I never told my parents about this or about my
fears. I felt sure that they would not let me go alone if I
did. But Martha was too busy to come with me, and Aunt
Elsa, like my parents, was afraid to leave her house so that
she could not come to us. I found my English lessons far
too fascinating to risk losing them.

The only other excursions away from home, where we
lived only in the rooms overlooking the back garden in
order to escape the flying glass of frequently shattered win-
dowpanes of our drawing room and my own bedroom,
which faced the street, were the occasions when I accompanied Martha to collect our food. For the whole of these
three months, until my mother and I left for England, we
were fed by the owners of several restaurants who were in
debt to my father for his legal services. Inns and restaurants
were an intrinsic part of my father's life. He had particular
corner tables always on reserve at some of them, and specific
meals of the week were regularly eaten at these tables. It
was one of the great treats of my childhood to accompany
my parents, and even more exciting to accompany my father
alone, on these occasions. Now, every day, Martha would
go to one or the other of these restaurants and return with
ready-cooked meals in oven-proof metal containers that sat
slotted on top of each other forming a kind of round tower.
Sometimes I accompanied her to the Hotel Römischer Kai-
ser (The Roman Emperor) or to the Gasthaus zum Grünen
Hirsch (At the Green Stag), where, our teachers impressed
on us, Beethoven had played the spinet during his flight

from the nearby castle at Grätz where he had composed the Apassionata Sonata. Whenever I went with Martha to collect these meals, I encountered red-faced, elderly innkeepers, whom I knew well as my father's friends and who, like my headmaster, were unable to meet my eyes.

Martha was the shield between us and the outside world. She not only helped with the usual household tasks. She went on errands to "the authorities," fetched our food, did the shopping, and negotiated with unwelcome visitors who came to the door. She did all this with kindness and an unconscious grace, always remembering to take my little dog, Struppel, with her so that he might have an outing. But her most heroic act, performed "as her Christian duty" regularly every morning for many months, was to go downstairs with a bucket and scrubbing brush at the crack of dawn. Then, in full sight of any passersby, and risking her own personal safety, she scrubbed graffiti like "Jewish swine" from the magnificent front door behind which we were more or less imprisoned.

It was Martha who, one night in December, opened the door at 3:00 A.M. to the group of six S.S. men who came to search our home. My parents and I were summoned and stood watching, in our dressing gowns, while the men tramped about the place opening cupboards and drawers. On finding my grandfather's Hebrew prayerbooks, Sabbath candlesticks, and menorah in the antique cupboard in our hall, they bundled them up to take them away and announced that we would have to come with them immediately. Then, while we stood there, quite stunned, they went into a huddle in a corner. One of the S.S. men was the son of Paula Heintz, a close friend of my parents. He had known our family well since he was a little boy. After conferring in their corner, the senior spokesman announced that they had changed their minds, and we could remain at home, but must leave the country by the first of March.

Like all other refugees, we would be allowed to take a few personal belongings and the equivalent of one dollar, in cash, out of the country. I have no memory of how, or whether, we returned to bed that night.

During the next weeks, there was much discussion about our future. The most exciting plan as far as I was concerned was the suggestion that we would have a milk round in England. For some reason, this seems to have been the only possibility that I heard about. Perhaps no others were discussed, or perhaps I was simply not privy to any others. In any case, I had wonderful visions of careering around the countryside, myself on top of the milk cart with my father driving the horses like those that delivered our milk at home. I saw myself jumping down from the cart having nice little chats with English servants and distributing liters of creamy milk into the waiting pots and carafes. This rosy vision never amounted to anything.

It turned out that the only work permitted to foreigners in England was domestic labor. My father, now in his early sixties, who knew no English, felt he could not commit himself to domestic service. But my mother, who had learned some English at school, was game, and it was decided that she and I would have to go alone to begin with. Advisers seemed to think that it would be easy enough for my mother to find work as a maid and keep me with her, and through friends of friends a vicar in a small Sussex village was approached who might be willing to help. Once in England she would search for an English sponsor to guarantee my father's economic survival, and when this had been achieved he would join us.

Preparations for our stay in England now went ahead at full speed. Friends in Vienna arranged that my mother and I would be ushered into England as guests of an English couple, the McCleans, who were even then wintering at an Austrian spa. This made it possible for us to enter Great Britain on a visitor's visa, the only type of visa still available at this time.

Our old seamstress, Fräulein Schmidt, spent a few days with us making several dresses—far too large—for me "to grow into." I am wearing one of these, a small white-and-navy check pattern with a white collar, in a photograph taken at my English school about two years later. It is obviously already much too small and stretched to the limit across my breasts. My mother packed carefully chosen items into a huge brown trunk, while I insisted on filling a large part of it with my favorite children's books.

Martha offered to look after my father when we had left. She also promised to take care of my dog, Struppel, and my canary, Pipsi, when my father left the country to join us.

The date of our departure was set for the end of January. We were to take the midnight express to Vienna and there to meet our English hosts and procure our visa from the British consulate. My father and Struppel accompanied my mother and me through the snowy streets to the railway station. I was nervous but buoyed up by the adventure before me. My parents were silent. The train glided in at ten minutes to midnight. We settled in the compartment with our hand luggage, my mother's jewelry hidden among our underclothes. I waved excitedly to my father, as he stood on the platform holding Struppel on a short lead. I never saw him again.

Not being used to staying up so late, I slept most of the long night journey to Vienna, and I was unaware of my mother's frame of mind. In fact, only on my thirty-eighth birthday, my mother's age at the time of this momentous night journey, did my conscience jolt me into attempting to place myself in my mother's shoes and to imagine what her feelings must have been throughout this period of her

life. From the journey itself, I remember only a fleeting fear
that the customs officials might discover the bits of jewelry
among our baggage and on our persons. But they seemed
uninterested in us, and we found ourselves in Vienna before
I was aware of it and quickly made our way to Ina Sobeck-
Skal's apartment.

When the Nazi troubles came upon us, our landlords,
the Sobeck-Skals, were kind and helpful. In the first place,
they offered to store our furniture when we fled to England.
Secondly, the baroness proposed that my mother and I
should stay in her Viennese apartment while waiting for
our British visa. My impression of this apartment is unforgettable. A small old woman had been advised of our arrival
and was waiting for us outside. She led us into the foyer
with its old-fashioned kitchen stove and then opened the
double doors into the main salon.

We had entered a shrine. The room was decorated in
dark red and gold. Walls, carpet, upholstery were all the
same deep crimson. The walls and every surface were covered
with portraits, photographs, or sculptures of the beautiful
and tragic Austrian Empress Elisabeth. A full-length life-
size oil painting of the empress in her riding habit hung on
the main wall opposite the door. At least two dozen smaller
portraits, miniatures, and photographs of Elisabeth, illuminated by small lamps or candles, stood upon side tables, on
the grand piano, and on special pedestals. My mother and
I were bemused but, knowing our baroness, also amused.

Our situation during this week in Vienna was precari-
ous. We had left my father behind in our hometown, hop-
ing that he would be able to follow us at a later date.
Meanwhile, my mother and I were supposedly being
escorted to England as the guests of the British McCleans,
who had been taking a cure in the mountains near Vienna.
We spent many hours waiting in the anterooms at the British consulate. When we were finally ushered into the pres-

ence of His Majesty's Consul, we faced a tall, unsmiling man who grudgingly agreed to sign the necessary papers. Those days in Baroness Ina's Vienna apartment have left me with confused and unreal memories. We slept in the midst of romantic, almost religious signs of worship of the charismatic empress who in 1896 had been stabbed to death by a fanatic anarchist. Outside we saw Nazi guards forcing well-dressed Jewish women to sweep the snow from the streets. Wedged between these scenes is the tight-lipped, impenetrable face of the British consul who held our lives in the balance.

PART II

AN EDUCATION
IN BRITAIN

CHAPTER
4

TWO WEEKS AFTER WE
arrived in England, my mother, now thirty-eight years old,
began her job as a maid to the family of the Reverend
Daunton-Fear in Lindfield. This picturesque Sussex village
consists of a long curved street leading from a duck pond
slightly uphill to the high steepled church. Even in 1939, at
the height of the depression, Lindfield looked prosperous.
Comfortably endowed middle-class people, quite a few of
them retired, inhabited most of its houses. The Reverend
Daunton-Fear's vicarage had grown out of a jumble of architectural periods and stood in a large garden opposite the
church.

My mother and I were given a servant's bedroom,
which was heated by a gas fire that popped and hissed
alarmingly. While it was easier to light than the majestic
tiled stoves that had graced our rooms at home, it gave us
neither their comfortable warmth nor their aesthetic security.
My mother said that since she was now the maid, she was
pleased not to have to clean out its grate, nor to carry the
coals, but I was appalled because unless one cowered within

two or three feet of this gas contraption with its bluish-pink flames, one hardly felt its warmth. Through these cold dark February mornings, we dressed close by the gas fire, warming our garments before it to escape their clamminess.

The Reverend Daunton-Fear was a tall, cheerful man with a booming voice and a hearty manner. His family consisted of his elegant, small, blond wife, who must have washed her hands constantly as she always smelled of Pears soap, and their two-year-old daughter, whose nurse, Cheggy, soon became a good friend and support to my mother. Mrs. Daunton-Fear had a little sitting room furnished with the first fitted carpet I had ever seen. Both the carpet and the upholstered furniture were a delicate Wedgwood green. It was in this room that all important decisions were made and announced. It was here that I was told that I would be going to St. Clair, a school in nearby Haywards Heath, first as a day girl, and later possibly as a boarder. It was in this room that my mother had to discuss her work and position with her new employers.

My mother never talked about the problem with me, but I could see that the Daunton-Fears, particularly Mrs. Daunton-Fear, were having trouble with their approach as employers of a servant who was so obviously their equal. My mother behaved just as she always did, very straightfor-wardly, but her carriage and her manner, despite her maid's uniform, belied her office, even had her situation not been known to the vicar and his wife. The situation was, of course, the reason why she had been employed in the first place. The Reverend Daunton-Fear was one of many English clergymen who answered the call to help Hitler's refugees.

My mother and I usually ate in the kitchen after she had served the vicar and his wife their meals in the dining room, but occasionally we had tea with the family in their large drawing room around the open coal fire. The little girl's nurse, Cheggy, played equally with me and her charge, and on Sunday mornings I accompanied the family to church, while my mother cleaned the house and helped the cook to prepare the Sunday lunch. I did not feel comfortable in the Lindfield vicarage, despite its charm and the warmth of its vicar.

A mysterious and happy presence who lived in a cottage behind the vicarage was "the deaconess." The deaconess, whose name I cannot remember, if I ever knew her by anything but her professional title, was a tall, somewhat angular woman with a beatific smile. One could catch glimpses of her long, soft blue gown as she glided like a moving delphinium past the vicarage. Deaconesses are supposed to be pastoral helpers to the clergy. They are expected to occupy themselves with the poor, the illiterate, the sick, and so forth. In retrospect, it does not seem to me that Lindfield or its surroundings offered our deaconess enough scope to carry out her mission. Perhaps this is why she had the time to occupy herself with me, to invite me to tea in her cottage with or without my mother, to take me for cocoa and cake at Araminta's, the village teashop, and to introduce me to various schoolgirls' storybooks. On second thought, perhaps, she was indeed carrying out her mission by bestowing her pastoral care on a refugee.

I was much struck by the Anglican service conducted by the Reverend Daunton-Fear when I accompanied the family to the church across the street. In the Lutheran church in Troppau, we had sat quietly through most of the service, standing up only once to say a prayer. The Catholic maids whom I had often accompanied to the Church of the Holy Ghost had spent much time crossing themselves and genuflecting as they entered and left the church. However, I had never been in a church where the congregation was expected to stand, sit, and kneel in such constant and busy rotation as we did in the church at Lindfield under our

vicar's direction. We seemed to bob up and down, shuffling
to and from our knees to sit in the pews and, before one
had collected oneself, standing up again to sing a hymn or
to recite a creed. Heads were bowed and quickly raised; old
and stiff knees creaked ominously. When my mother
wanted to take me for a walk on Sunday afternoon, I
objected that I had had more exercise in church than during
a lesson in gymnastics. I have since wondered whether the
busy Anglican services were devised to counteract the horrendous damp cold of English churches, which supposedly
saved the old stonework from deterioration. The recent
installation of central heat radiators surely comforts the congregation, but now the ancient stones and wooden ceilings
are suffering.

The first Saturday morning after we arrived in Lindfield, the vicar drove my mother and me to Haywards
Heath to talk to Miss Stevens, the headmistress of St. Clair's
School for Girls. I thought that this expedition was to see
whether this would be a suitable place for me. Miss Stevens
talked mostly to me, asking many questions about my life
at home and the sorts of things I had done in school before.
In fact I was being examined, but in such a subtle manner
that I did not understand that I was passing or perhaps
failing an examination. I did not then realize that my
education at this school would have to be Miss Stevens's
gift to me, as St. Clair was her private business and, in
order to attend, all other pupils paid fees. We were taken
on a tour of the school, Miss Stevens walking in front
holding my hand, my mother and the Reverend Daunton-
Fear following on behind. I was astonished to discover
that this building, which appeared to be, and in fact was,
a comfortable large private house set in delightful gardens
with fishponds and bridges, a tennis court, a small rhododendron wood and orchards, also included classrooms, a

gymnastics room, and a laboratory. I had never seen or imagined a school like this.

The interview took place in Miss Stevens's personal sitting room in an upstairs corner of the house. Its windows looked across an oval lawn and tennis court and beyond the garden fence onto a public park and cricket ground. The room was filled with flowers, chintz-covered easy chairs, and personal mementoes, a small replica of the Venus de Milo from Miss Stevens's Italian journey, and her pictures of Norwegian fjords, about which she waxed lyrical at the slightest provocation. The bookshelves housed her collection of poetry, including her favorite war poets, Blunden, Owen, and Sassoon. I came to know this room extremely well over the next few years, but on that day in February 1939, I simply felt that I was in the presence of comforting benevolence. "When would you like to start?" Miss Stevens asked.

As headmistress, Miss Stevens was by no means a nominal head of her school. She was the central and dominant figure. She directed the whole establishment. She chose both the teaching and domestic staff. She interviewed parents and pupils, and she looked after the domestic arrangements and the meals and oversaw the grounds and gardeners. She taught many classes to senior girls. She kissed the boarders good-night and was concerned about their emotional as well as their physical well-being.

After the end of my first term at St. Clair, Miss Stevens decided it would be better if I became a boarder while my mother continued her domestic service in various English households. I thus began to live in this wonderful house, not only during the term, but also over the long vacations. Throughout my schoolyears with her, I thought of Miss Stevens in her capacity of headmistress, as did the other girls. I realized that I was not in the same position, and that

I was treated somewhat differently from the other children, especially in the holidays, when she and I remained alone in the house with the servants, but as none of the others made me feel that I was receiving special favors, I managed to ignore this fact.

Haywards Heath, the home of St. Clair's School for Girls, was a rather sleepy provincial town on the main Southern Railway line about thirty-five miles south of London on the way to Brighton. Roughly a hundred pupils, including the little ones in the kindergarten and a handful of us boarders, attended the school. The girls at St. Clair were the daughters of the local middle-middle class, a few London or Brighton business commuters, shopkeepers, professional men like dentists, photographers, and farmers from the surrounding Sussex countryside. The latter came into Haywards Heath by bus from such nearby villages as Ardingly, Handcross, Balcombe, or Horsted Keynes.

Very early on, I discovered that learning to speak English was going to be complicated by the fact that many of the children, particularly those coming in from the farms, spoke with an accent of which Miss Stevens strongly disapproved. "Girls," she would say, "you will never get a job with the BBC." Not only did she have to deal with my confusion over *v*'s and *w*'s, grapple with *th*, and correct the mispronunciation I had acquired from my Aunt Elsa in Troppau, who had taught me to pronounce sounds like *u* in "but" as "boet." She also had to fight Sussex vowels akin to cockney, which I digested happily as kindly local girls taught me new words and phrases.

I was amazed by the gentleness of these girls. My school experiences in and out of the classroom in Czechoslovakia had tended largely to competition. In contrast, these English children seemed to be determined to help and encourage each other. The most remarkable and frequent occurrence, which surprised me anew each time it happened, was that the girls apologized if they knocked into me during a vigorous game of netball.

The mistresses also surprised me by their openness. Without exception it was the rule that if a girl did not understand something during a lesson she simply put up her hand and asked to have it explained. And the teacher would explain until the questioner was satisfied. In my Czech schools we would not have dared to interrupt a teacher in class. Whatever we did not understand had to be sorted out at home or among ourselves. Nevertheless, I must have been a great nuisance in class with my interminable "What does it mean?" During my second week at St. Clair, Miss Wiltshire, a friendly Canadian mistress, presented me with a tiny English dictionary, which, to everyone's great amusement, I wore like a pendant on a cord around my neck.

One of the first things that happened when I became a pupil at St. Clair was that a uniform was found for me. We wore navy blue wraparound serge skirts, which gave us more freedom while running, and tomato red jerseys with small collars closed by two white pearl buttons at the neck. In the summer we wore pink-and-white-flowered cotton frocks. It was an unusually noninstitutional-looking uniform in contrast to the tunics, long-sleeved shirt blouses, and neckties of other schools. Of course, we did wear the usual large-brimmed black velour hats with the St. Clair initials, STC, woven into an emblem on the hatband. The uniforms were ordered from an outfitters in Brighton, but Miss Stevens found several mothers of girls who had outgrown their skirts and jerseys who were willing to pass them on to me. I was told that a uniform had been found for me and was very proud to wear it. As I had never worn a uniform before, this was something rather exciting. I did not realize for a long time that other children had to buy their own. As time went on, the uniform also became extremely useful as it hid the fact that my own clothes were quickly becoming far too small and shabby and we had no money to replace them. Miss Stevens herself bought and presented me with my very own new school hat. She also found other hand-me-down clothes for me over the years. One time she produced a splendid deep blue velvet dress with dozens of little velvet buttons down the front, which I wore even after it was far too short and tight, because I had become so fond of it. Later, as the war progressed and clothes were rationed, there was little shame in wearing other children's castoffs; even people with money did not have enough clothing coupons to buy new dresses when they needed them.

Miss Stevens taught both literature and mathematics to senior forms. Through some kind of osmosis, we believed or knew that she had lost her sweetheart during the First World War. This, we assumed, was why she was so intrigued by the war poets and made us read them frequently with great attention.

Robin, Miss Stevens's little white West Highland Scottie, took practically an equal share in running the school. Wherever we saw Robin, Miss Stevens was sure to be close by. If we tried to sneak past her study, her bedroom, or the bathroom in the middle of the night, for example, Robin's presence outside the door would quickly alert us to her whereabouts. During lessons Robin was part of the class. No one who was ever in her classroom can forget her writing algebraic formulae on the blackboard with Robin tucked neatly under her left arm. While Miss Stevens presided over morning assembly and prayers, Robin sat quietly by her side, facing the entire school. If, as occasionally happened, Miss Stevens's upper teeth dropped while she sang the morning hymn too vigorously, Robin was more embarrassed than we girls, who waited for this moment with happy anticipation. At the end of assembly, Robin led the procession, waddling after Miss Stevens on his short sturdy legs, as staff and pupils followed on their way to their different classrooms.

Every morning after breakfast, and again before afternoon tea, we boarders were expected to take Robin for a half-hour walk. Depending on the season and the weather, we stretched or shortened this half hour most creatively. We had our favorite walks. Sometimes we went around the cricket ground or in the direction of nearby villages like Lindfield or Cuckfield; sometimes we went up Broadway past the cinema, where we could check out the display of stills of our filmstar heroes, and on to the main shopping street, to wander around Woolworth.

Miss Stevens's study was a large rectangular room that included not only her desk, a grandfather clock, two comfortable wing chairs, Robin's basket, and the brass coal scuttle by the fireplace, but also the long mahogany table at which she, the other mistresses, and the boarding pupils breakfasted and dined. If the senior class was small enough, its instruction also took place around the dining table. This study/dining room was the hub of the school. As it served so many different functions, most happenings of importance occurred there; and as I lived in the school both as a pupil and as a sort of foster child, I spent a great deal of time in the room in both capacities. I liked it best in the winter when a comfortable fire burned in the grate, and in the early spring when a wonderful rose-colored japonica bush flowered just outside the large floor-to-ceiling sash window.

I loved the English breakfasts we were served, even in wartime. Fried bread covered with fried tomatoes on Marmite for example or baked beans on toast were favorite starts to the day. At suppertime we often became unruly, and there was a sequence of evenings when we watched the grandfather clock and, punctually to the minute, began that helpless adolescent giggling that is so uncomfortable for both the victim and her audience. Miss Stevens hardly ever reprimanded our giggling, which must have driven the mistresses quite mad. Some of the younger staff members usually brought us to order when they had had enough.

Miss Stevens had an amusingly prim way of dealing with unmentionable problems. If Robin made a bad smell, one of his less endearing traits, she would tell one of us to remove the "odoriferous" beast immediately. Whenever the toilet of the daygirls' cloakroom next to the study-dining room flushed unmistakably while we were entertaining visitors, she would exclaim, "Isn't the birdsong splendid this year!"

Our first sight of Miss Stevens was early in the morning if we caught her slipping from her bedroom to the bathroom, her nineteen-twenties bobbed white hair only slightly ruffled, in her dressing-gown without her teeth, carrying her daily glass of boiling hot water, which she drank religiously for "medicinal purposes." Our last awareness of her late at night was seeing Robin stationed outside the study door. One or the other of us boarders would creep down the stairs to the hallstand outside the study. Here she placed the graded pile of homework exercise books or tests. Many a night we lay abed in panicstricken anxiety worrying about these homework books, unable to wait until morning to discover how we had done. If the books were there, we quickly riffled through them and dashed upstairs if we saw Robin prick up his ears. Miss Stevens's marginal notes were usually witty and encouraging. One of her better efforts was her ironic attack on my spelling when, on my math homework dealing with isosceles triangles, she wrote, "Unfortunately for you, Susanna, there are no angels in geometry!"

It was Miss Stevens who taught me some unforgettable new habits and modes of behavior. In her opinion, two of my most glaring Continental offenses were staring at people and "speaking with my hands." Staring was rude, she said; it interfered with others' privacy. Gesturing with one's hands signified an inability to express oneself verbally. One must learn to use words so effectively that they were the most important part of communication. I have never quite mastered the injunction not to stare—especially at people who attract me. However, I will sit on my hands rather than use them while speaking and am painfully conscious of others' gesturing during a discussion.

During the vacations I was well occupied. Often, Miss Stevens, whose father had been the editor and publisher of the *Mid-Sussex Times*, took me visiting her friends and relations: her sister, who had married a farmer near Horsham, and her brother, a bank manager in London's Edgware Road. Sometimes we visited an old friend of her father's in Lindfield. I didn't care too much for these particular visits. The old gentleman used to hold my hand and stroke my legs as we sat drinking tea in his rooms, and when we said goodbye he insisted on presenting me with wet and nasty kisses.

For Christmas Day I usually accompanied Miss Stevens to some special friends of hers in Brighton, where we had an elegant and traditional meal with gifts for me from all those present. Here I first encountered the traditional English Christmas fare, so different from the carp, the goose, and the baked goods like cookies and *Strietzel* we used to have at home. I thought the turkey rather bland, and the plum pudding, despite the threepenny bits to be found in it, was not nearly as delicious as the *Vanillenkipferln* with hazelnuts and the fig roll that I watched our cook produce a few weeks before Christmas at home.

During the spring and summer holidays, Miss Stevens found me special jobs in the garden and grounds to keep me from getting bored. The most delightful and memorable of these was painting the school gates. The main gate was at the end of a very long rhododendron drive leading from one of Haywards Heath's major roads. It was a gate large enough for cars to drive through, and on several occasions I painted it a rich bright blue. I made the job last as long as possible; it was fun to be so occupied in the driveway when visitors or tradesmen appeared. Moreover, the thick blue paint flowed smoothly from my brush onto the wide slats of the gate and dried with a lovely glossy shine. Once through the front gate and inside the school grounds, the drive curved around a large daffodil meadow with a couple of apple trees to the paved netball court in front of the house. Another drive led from Sydney Street to the back gate, which I once painted bright green and on another occasion a lovely shiny black. I was extremely proud and possessive of "my" gates and used to be furious if any of the girls, or some car, scratched or disfigured them in any way.

Sometimes I was invited to tea or supper at the home of one or the other of the daygirls. On one occasion, when I was happily ensconced having tea with my friend Joyce at the other end of town, the house shook and we heard a heavy dull thud. Almost immediately afterwards the phone rang and Joyce's mother said that Miss Stevens was asking for me to come home. I was taken back to school rather abruptly. I found Miss Stevens waiting for me at the gate with Robin in her arms and a bandage on her head. Very alarmed, I ran to her and she led me wordlessly into the study/dining room where she had been having her tea with Robin asleep in his basket. The window was shattered, and broken glass lay everywhere, both in the room and outside in the garden. A German bomber hit by ack-ack guns had gone to ground and exploded with his unused bombs in the Sussex countryside. Miss Stevens and I survived this incident without too much of a trauma. But poor little

Robin was extremely shaken and frightened of loud noise for the rest of his life.

Strange as this may seem, this particular bomb incident was the closest I ever came personally to an air raid throughout the entire war. By some mixture of luck and protective foresight on the part of my mother and her friends, I moved about England and Wales several times, always escaping the worst of the bombings in other parts of the British Isles.

At the end of my second term at St. Clair, that is during the winter of 1939, Miss Stevens's banker brother insisted that she must draw in her reins, spend less money, and be less generous with the free education she bestowed on those who could not afford to pay. Very unhappily, she told me that I would have to go to another school.

The Reverend Daunton-Fear, my mother's first employer, came to the rescue and found an Anglican convent school in Leigh-on-Sea, in Essex, where, with his recommendation, I would be welcome as a non-fee-paying pupil. St. Michael's was a small school, run by Anglican nuns in the charge of a pleasant but remote Mother Superior.

I arrived in Leigh-on-Sea just after the Christmas holidays and soon announced to my mother that the place should be renamed Leigh-on-Mud. Leigh is a small residential town near the popular seaside resort of Southend, though it was hard to imagine why anyone should wish to spend any time there. The place was cold, gray, and windy. When it did not rain, the cold spray from the distant sea filled the air. Even so, the sea hardly ever came in close enough so that one might enjoy the sight of water, and the mud was all pervasive. Supervised by one of the nuns, we girls from St. Michael's used to walk in crocodile file for what seemed like hours along the promenade overlooking the mud.

The atmosphere of the school, like the shore of Leigh-on-Sea, was gray. The nuns in their dark habits always in evidence, teaching, supervising, cooking, and presiding at meals, were a source of morbid curiosity. Somehow we never resolved the question of whether or not their heads had been shaved. Sometime during my stay at St. Michael's, most of the girls and a number of the nuns contracted German measles. When we were better, some of us were allowed to visit one of the most friendly and cheerful of the nuns in her sickroom. We hoped to solve the mystery of the possibly nonexistent hair, but alas, Sister Lucy's head was covered after all.

Twice a day, after breakfast and after supper, and three times on Sundays, we attended chapel, wearing small white cotton veils with colored bands according to our age and status. The veil acted as an intriguing addition to my wardrobe for about a week. After that the whole thing began to pall. I tried to discover how the other girls felt about this constant praying, but they were either quite ribald about it or too, too pious, and I couldn't decide whether anyone felt as bewildered as I.

The girls at St. Michael's were mostly the daughters of lower civil servants who were stationed in the colonies. The school was minimally equipped and the living accommodation sparse and ugly. We slept in long dormitories with beds divided from each other by white curtains and had to wait much too long to get into the bathroom or lavatory, as there were very few. After supper, and during free afternoons on weekends, we all huddled together around a piano, on which a pretty, blond, older girl who smelled unpleasantly of something I couldn't identify played the latest dance tunes. Later I realized that the unpleasant odor was stale menstrual blood—a memory forever connected to this occasion.

Every evening also, we gathered around the radio to listen to the news and some of the topical, but more cheerful entertainment like Tommy Handley and *Monday Night at Eight*. Much of the pleasure of these comedians went straight over my head. My English was not up to their cockney accents, and my knowledge of England was too new to understand their witty allusions. Neither the other girls nor the nuns were able to explain things adequately.

Moreover, my introduction to Leigh-on-Sea was hardly enhanced by the news from the war. During this spring of 1940, while I was cloistered at St. Michael's, Hitler advanced on all fronts with relentless speed. Night after night, as we sat by our wireless, we were bombarded with ever more frightening bulletins. In swift succession the Germans overran Denmark, Norway, Holland, Belgium, and Luxembourg. Finally, late in May, the British army had to evacuate Dunkirk. Young as we were, we understood that the paeans of patriotic praise for the brilliance of the evacuation and the courage of the innumerable little fishing boats that brought back tired and wounded soldiers were simply a blind for disaster. My letters transmitting my dislike of the school cannot have cheered my mother, who was surely far more disturbed by these German successes than I.

One morning the Mother Superior called me into her office. She announced in her usual quiet and dignified tones that she had had letters from my mother and from Miss Stevens of St. Clair. I had been invited to stay in Haywards Heath for the summer holidays and thereafter I was to remain at St. Clair. I burst into tears of relief, and would have hugged her, except that one does not hug a nun.

From the moment that I became a pupil at St. Clair until I left three and a half years later, I fell completely under its spell. Not only Miss Stevens, the headmistress, but also the other mistresses helped to introduce me to the strangeness of English boarding school life. As a team the mistresses at St. Clair were a disparate lot. One or two of them usually lived in the school; the others came in by the day from Haywards Heath or the surrounding country. Mrs. Glennister, who taught music, came from as far away as Brighton.

My favorites were Miss Wiltshire and Miss Moilliet, who lived in the school when I first arrived in 1939. Miss Wiltshire, a Canadian from Nova Scotia, loved England in what I later came to recognize as a typically colonial way. She liked the romance of its history learned from her parents, grandparents, and her own school days, but would have preferred the Canadian amenities. She was somewhat scathing about English bathrooms, cold and draughty bedrooms and corridors, and was the first to huddle around the comfortable coke-burning stove in the room we used for tea and homework. I felt a great affinity for her perhaps because I also missed the greater physical comforts I had left behind. It was Miss Wiltshire who made the greatest efforts to improve my English as fast as possible, while Miss Stevens was more concerned with getting me to speak correctly. Between them they managed to spur me on so that I was proficient fairly quickly—something that was wonderfully helpful in making me feel less strange.

Miss Moilliet, whose name, Maida, I found intriguing, was a softly spoken and mannered woman who had a special warmth and charm. Her hair constantly escaped its careless arrangement, and she had none of Miss Wiltshire's brisk energy. She taught us French. I had already quite a start on that language, having learned it with my mother's friend Joanna in Troppau. Miss Moilliet seemed to approve of my pronunciation, which was indeed very different from that of the English girls' many false starts.

Miss Wiltshire and Miss Moilliet used to like taking us boarders on excursions to the county town of Lewes, where we roamed around the old castle and visited Anne of Cleve's house. But most wonderful were our picnics on the windswept downs, those smooth, rolling, green hills nuzzled by black-nosed sheep, so very different from anything I had ever known before. There was something deeply comforting and yet adventurous about these downs, and we clamored often to go back to Lewes and if possible to wander over Firle Beacon. Many years later I had other connections to Lewes and Firle, and the special greenness of Sussex, whether it is the luxurious trees surrounding Lindfield and Ardingly, or the soft bare roundness of the downs, has remained at the core of the meaning of Englishness for me.

Miss Daitches taught the kindergarten and was less colorful than the other mistresses, at least for us children. But one morning, as I was working at my usual before-breakfast piano practice, hammering away at the hymn I was to play for school prayers, Miss Stevens burst into the room, her hair standing up on end, as upset as I had ever seen her, and ordered me to stop playing immediately. I assumed my playing had reached an all-time low and only slowly comprehended that my offense was connected to the fact that Miss Daitches's father had died the night before. The hymn I was murdering, "Oh God Our Help in Ages Past," was a traditional funeral hymn, and Miss Stevens considered my banging away at it while poor Miss Daitches was packing her bags on the floor above me, to return home for her father's funeral, in the worst of taste.

The children also accepted me in their midst with the least possible fuss and a certain amount of pleased curiosity. Very quickly, I felt at home. I was somewhere in the middle of the school; the little ones, if they thought about me at all, were in awe of a stranger in their midst; the older ones treated me like a little pet; and my own age group soon dealt with me as an equal. At least that's how it felt. I don't know what went on behind the scenes. Perhaps they were all given a lecture on how to behave with a refugee. If so, I was never aware of it. Occasionally, someone asked me why I was a refugee. When I tried to explain about Hitler and the four Jewish grandparents, they would say, "But you aren't a bit Jewish," and while I didn't know what they meant by this statement, it didn't disturb me, particularly because I didn't see how one can wear one's religion on one's sleeve. Much, much later it dawned on me that what these children had meant by Jewish was their image of poor East End Jewish Londoners or a sort of Shylock.

It soon became evident that, except for English language and literature, I was somewhat in advance of the girls of my age, which made up for the liberties I took with their language. At the same time, my mispronunciations and poor prose style and my more than quaint spelling detracted from any cleverness I might have exhibited. One-upmanship was not the order of the day.

One of the more complex institutions for me to assimilate was the concept of "houses." If St. Clair had been a large boarding school, the pupils would have lived in several houses, each with its own housemistress and prefects, that interesting English arrangement whereby the children police themselves. As St. Clair occupied only one house, we were divided into groups, which were metaphorically known as houses. Each house was represented by its own color, and we wore the colors of our house in the form of a button-brooch on our jerseys or summer frocks. Even more confusing was the fact that these "houses" were known by the names of English queens. Queen Anne House was yellow; Queen Elizabeth, dark blue; and Queen Mary (for Mary Tudor) dark green. As the girls delighted in calling her "Bloody Mary," this compounded the confusion. On my arrival I was immediately assigned to Queen Mary, but it took a while before I grasped the concept. What it meant, of course, was that I was expected to learn about loyalty, about belonging to a group, and about team spirit.

We played games in our house teams, but, luckily for me, sport was not one of St. Clair's more important concerns. I soon learned to hit the tennis balls over the net. I even helped to work the little machine that drew the chalk lines whenever they had been erased by the rain or the lawn mower. In winter we were all expected to play netball, and since I was tall I was quickly put into goal, which excused me from having to run around the court. I managed to shoot the baskets quite easily, so it was never too obvious how much I disliked games and how much I would rather have sat indoors and read a nice book.

As I had no brothers or sisters, I was enchanted by the variety of children around me at all times. To share a bedroom with one or two other girls was a treat. While our maid Liese had slept on the couch in my bedroom at home, she had come to bed hours after I was asleep and risen long before I was awake in order to start cleaning and to light the stoves. Now I had girls with whom to gossip at night, which was the best time for exchanging confidences. Moreover, there was someone to warn me when I read with my flashlight and one of the mistresses did her rounds to check on us. At home, when I had read in bed, my mother had frequently caught me unawares.

During my years at St. Clair, we numbered somewhere between four and six boarders. While we had our breakfast and our supper and weekend meals in the study/dining room, lunch was eaten in the science room next to the kitchen, with the group of daygirls who came from the surrounding countryside. The most delicious new dishes I discovered in England were the puddings. Custard was a revelation! Fruit pies with custard, and steamed or boiled puddings, particularly jam pudding or spotted dick (a suet pudding with dates or raisins), also eaten with thick Bird's Custard, were my favorites. Soggy cabbage and strong-smelling cod were less appealing. Afternoon tea, consisting of cucumber, fish-, or meatpaste sandwiches and a slice of cake, was taken with the mistress on duty. In summer we had our tea on the terrace above the steps leading to the lawn and tennis court. But most of the year we had tea around the glowing, slow-burning coke stove in the kindergarten room, where, sitting on the tiny children's chairs, we also listened to the radio after doing our homework in the evening. It was here that we heard most of the dramatic announcements charting the course of the war.

The youngest boarder, Miss Stevens's niece Janet, was six when I was thirteen. A mischievous little girl when she arrived, she amused all of us. Various older and younger girls boarded occasionally for short periods while their parents settled into the area. My most constant companion, just a couple of years younger than I, was a girl called Nan with a mysteriously missing father. I learned much later that her parents had met on shipboard, married in haste, and separated very soon after Nan was born. But this was never talked about. Nan's mother was very tall, thin, and angular and reminded me of a jumping horse. She lived, appropriately, in the village of Maresfield together with Nan's grandmother, where during the holidays I was sometimes invited to stay.

Nan's grandmother was an extremely proper old lady. In her house everything had to be done just so—our conversations as polished as the silver. There was a prissiness about this old lady that set my teeth on edge, but I could not define it. Nan's mother, on the other hand, was warm and full of fun. We were not supposed to talk about our bodies or bodily functions. Behavior at table was strictly monitored, even more so than at school. Hands must be placed beside the plate on the table, not left on laps, as I had been taught to do at home. Forks, always held in the left hand, were turned convex side up and the food stacked on top of this convex curve; again, just the opposite from what I had done at home. Even peas must be balanced on the convex curve of the fork and somehow got up to one's mouth—a feat that took many months of training before I could achieve it. Fortunately, or perhaps unfortunately, there was much opportunity for practice since peas were one of the most popular English vegetables, to be served alternately with cabbage. Even so, we children preferred peas to the more nauseating "swedes," as the English call rutabagas, which appeared with increasing regularity once the war had begun.

It was at Nan's grandmother's house that I tried to knit a little blanket of pink and gray squares as a Christmas present for my mother's feet. Nan's mother and grandmother used a very different knitting method from the one I had been taught at home. I found the English method very clumsy and complained bitterly, when I got back to St. Clair, to Miss Wiltshire, who said there was no reason why I shouldn't knit according to the Continental method. She and Miss Moilliet experimented for a while until they discovered how it was done and then helped me to re-learn it.

Nan and I also created the imaginary games I had played through most of my earlier childhood. We became imaginatively ever more sophisticated, weaving long novels that lasted the entire term, in which we played the parts of all major and minor characters. Some sections of these novels we made into drama, and dragooning Miss Stevens's little dog, Robin, as well as other players from among the boarders, we gave public performances to the mistresses at weekends. I still have a formal acknowledgment from Miss Stevens, in which she answered us correctly, in the third person, writing that, "Miss Stevens is delighted to accept the invitation" to be present at one of these performances. A photograph shows Nan, Janet, and myself dressed in silks and velvet jackets, elegantly trimmed hats and high heels in exaggerated poses as three fashionable ladies with their small lapdog. Even my hair is magnificently curled on both sides. I had somehow managed to get hold of one curler and used it alternately each night, so that I usually looked quite lopsided with one side of my head splendidly curled and the other obstreperously dead straight.

In my next to last year at St. Clair, as the eldest boarder, I was given my own tiny bedroom next to Miss Stevens's room. I treasured my new privacy and the lovely view over the garden and the curve of the cricket ground. But I also missed the companionship of the other girls at night. However, we soon remedied this defect. After lights out, having made sure that Miss Stevens was still working in her study downstairs, Nan would creep along the corridors and slip into my bed so that we might continue our interesting conversations and develop the current dramatic improvisation. As in my much earlier childhood, with my friend Ilse, we acted out the passionate love scenes of our stories, Nan always playing the role of the male hero. But now the game had taken on a more real dimension. Neither Nan's respectable grandmother, nor Miss Stevens, nor my own mother would have been pleased to know how we spent many a night in that delightful little bedroom.

Several of the day girls were particularly significant in my school career. Audrey, the youngest daughter of a local dentist, was in my class, and, although she was extremely shy, we became friends. Her parents frequently invited me to come to tea on Sunday. This tea was nothing like the afternoon tea we had at school, nor like the *Jause* we had had at home. It was in fact a high tea, but I did not yet understand the intricate hierarchy of English meals. I only knew that it was a wonderful meal, the table loaded with many different types of food: sausages, sausage rolls, tinned salmon, bread and butter, salads, jam and treacle tarts, and all kinds of large and small cakes.

Audrey had three older sisters who were, or had been, pupils at St. Clair. All four of them had tight natural curls, which I found fascinating since my hair was so completely and boringly straight. They had exotic names like Daphne, the eldest, and Cicely, three years older than I, who was in her last year when I arrived. Cicely was tall and blond, and, perhaps because of her tight blond curls and the musical lilt to her name, I was completely bewitched by her. I tried to find her during recesses. I presented her with bunches of flowers picked surreptitiously in the garden. I even sent her poems, copied from my *Book of English Verse*. Whenever possible I passed by the upstairs cloakroom where senior girls kept their hats, coats, gym shoes, books, and notebooks. When I appeared, Cicely and her group of older girls giggled at my sheep's eyes and my offerings, but they did it in such a friendly way that I never felt disparaged. To my own, and probably everyone's, relief, this phase finally wore off, and I diverted my attentions to the filmstar who played the most romantic parts in the movies we were allowed to attend.

The two cinemas in Haywards Heath vied with each other to bring us the most patriotic pictures, trying to quell any despondency people might reasonably feel at the course of the war. Thus we saw movies such as Charlie Chaplin's hilarious impersonation of Hitler; and such romantic films as *The Sea Hawk* and *Elizabeth and Essex*, both about England's successes at the time of the Armada, which was a favorite school history topic, and featured that irresistible hero Errol Flynn. My friend Sheila was more enamored of David Niven, but both of us and most of the girls at St. Clair were enchanted by Leslie Howard, who portrayed to perfection the Scarlet Pimpernel, spiriting French refugees from under the noses of the revolutionary villains, a story we knew practically by heart. We were quite unaware that our archetypal English hero, Leslie Howard, was in fact Hungarian. Sheila and I wrote to our respective filmstar heroes asking for photographs, and each of us received handsome, autographed portraits after waiting for many weeks.

One morning I found a typewritten letter addressed to me and signed by Errol Flynn, telling me how much he appreciated my admiration. I was ecstatic, though I thought it a little strange that he should take the trouble. I examined the envelope, the typing, the signature. It was all quite different from the letters I normally received, and yet it was not quite what I would have expected from a Hollywood star. The envelope was pale blue, the stamp was American, but the postmark crooked and broken as though it had been pushed out of shape. The signature was more or less the same as that on the photograph. I wandered about showing my treasure to my closest friends and even some of the mistresses. Everyone oohed and aahed. Gradually, it dawned on me that someone had played a trick on me, and eventually I discovered that the culprit was Sheila's mother.

Sheila had arrived in Haywards Heath with her mother as a sort of private evacuee from London bombs. She was not billeted on a family, which was the usual practice with evacuees; instead she and her mother lived in rented rooms in the town. Her father, who worked in a bank, remained in London and occasionally came down to visit them. Sheila's mother took us out for walks and to the cinema. I also had tea or supper in their rooms, and we often played all sorts of board games together. I vividly remember Sheila's mother—a beautiful, dark, well-rounded woman sitting hunched over the Snakes and Ladders board and her disturbing manner of caressing her breast. Sheila was my age, and we quickly became fast friends and continued to work our way through to the senior form in tandem. We both became prefects of our houses, she of Queen Anne, I of Queen Mary, and in our last year shared the position of head girl, because Miss Stevens could not bring herself to favor one of us.

The office of head girl involved, among other duties, ringing the bell between classes. This ordinary large brass bell with a wooden handle was kept under the stand in the front hall, and five minutes before the end of each class, either Sheila or I left our lesson and trotted about the building, ringing it vigorously. This offered opportunities for all kinds of extracurricular activities, like conveying notes to people in their coats in the cloak room, messages to mistresses in other classrooms, even cadging a bite of something exciting from the kitchen, where the fat cook, Edith, occasionally condescended to be kind.

In the summer of 1942, Sheila and I had come as far as St. Clair could take us academically. We both sat for the Oxford school certificate, with Miss Stevens hovering nervously and worrying about our inadequacies. She thought that I would have difficulty in passing the examinations, particularly in history and English. In fact, we both did rather well. Sheila claimed I must be "a positive genius," because I had managed to surpass Miss Stevens's expectations. She herself went on to study mathematics, and I, who wanted to work with humanities, left for the Croydon High School, where I would be able to prepare for a university in the sixth form.

While all the mistresses at this school were deeply interested in our academic progress and hoped that we girls, and particularly Sheila and I, who were closer to leaving school, would continue our education at some higher level, it is surprising to me in retrospect that none of them prodded or inspired us in any way towards a career. Considering that none of these women were married or likely to be married in the future, and that they earned their living by teaching fairly contentedly as far as I could see, it would have been natural for them to ensure that we prepared ourselves for life realistically. Did they really expect that for each of us a prince would come? Was it simply not done to assume that a middle-class girl could possibly remain unmarried? The only memory I have of any mention of a career was Miss Stevens's irritation with me on one occasion when I queried some point during a discussion of a Shakespeare play in class—and she accused me of thinking like a lawyer. I remember exactly where I sat at that moment, so this must have made a deep impression on me.

We had only been in England for five weeks when Miss Stevens began to speak mournfully of the "Ides of March." I knew nothing of Julius Caesar, nor did I understand the complexity of her irony. She was thinking not of Brutus, or Cassius, but of Hitler's occupation of Prague on that fifteenth of March in 1939. My mother, however, understood it only too well. A little while earlier, in Lindfield's vicarage garden, she had told me that my father had left Troppau and the Sudetenland and was now living safely with some cousins in Prague. But with the Nazis in Prague, and in control of the whole of Czechoslovakia, time was running out for my father. It was clear that she would have to act very fast to be able to find the necessary sponsor to guarantee his support in England.

Throughout this time, he wrote me frequent, cheerful, and comforting letters expressing his expectation of our being reunited. He wrote that he was learning English, which was a difficult thing to do from a book. He wanted detailed descriptions of my daily life at school and was happy that I had found such a welcoming niche in my boarding school; he seemed to know me extremely well as the letters urged me over and over again not to neglect my body. Physical exercise, one of my least favorite occupations, would make me strong. "I have no worries about your schoolwork, but I am worried about your health," he wrote. When I did write to him about the games of "stool-ball" (a special Sussex version of cricket) that I had been playing, he replied that he had asked everyone he could think of, but that no one had any idea what this might be. He was interested in the books I read and asked if the film of *Tom Sawyer* that I had seen was as good as the book. Mischievously, he reminded me of the occasions when he and I wanted to play the card game Black Cat and prodded my mother into playing with us against her will. He urged me to write to him as he was unable to occupy himself with his professional activities and therefore spent many hours walking about the town and innumerable afternoons playing bridge and talking with friends and acquaintances about the problems that beset them. He wrote that there was no news from Troppau: "It is as though the place was completely obliterated, and my circle of acquaintances here is gradually diminishing—people disappear quite suddenly, one never knows what has become of them." Only very occasionally was there a sentence or two about how much patience was needed to wait for the longed-for permit to come to England.

My mother's first English position as a maid in Lindfield, close to my school in Haywards Heath, ended fairly soon after the Germans marched into Prague. I was not sure of the reasons for the change, but suspected that perhaps she had only been employed to give her an occupation and that the Reverend Daunton-Fear's vicarage did not really need another maid. However, I was not happy when, as we walked among the daffodils, she told me that she would soon be moving to another post, this time in the neighboring county of Surrey. She would no longer be within walking distance when I became a boarder at St. Clair.

And so, from the beginning of our life in England until 1942, that is throughout the years that I was at St. Clair, my mother was employed at some level of domestic service, as this was the only gainful occupation legally permitted to aliens in Britain. From my point of view, she seemed to move quite often from job to job, but in fact she was employed in only four different households.

Throughout her first few months, my mother tried hard to find a sponsor to guarantee the necessary affidavit to bring my father to England. After many false starts, and what must have been a painful and humiliating experience, she eventually found such a guarantor. Unfortunately, by the time she had achieved this difficult task the Germans had marched into Poland and war had broken out.

My mother was no longer close by when, on the momentous morning of Sunday, September 3, we did not, as usual, pile into Miss Stevens's small Austin Seven and drive to Lindfield church. Instead, we remained at St. Clair and in the flower-filled upstairs sitting room listened to Neville Chamberlain announce that we were now at war with Germany. His words left us with ominous and ambivalent feelings, which were quickly heightened when the sirens wailed loudly and, grabbing our gas masks in their little brown cardboard boxes, we ran downstairs into the school cellar.

Almost never did my mother speak about her second job as house/parlormaid to the Honorable Mrs. Ellesmere, at Englefield Green in Surrey. I gathered later from hearing her compare notes with our chemist friend, Tante Grete, who began her own English refugee life as a maid in Bristol, that she wore a maid's uniform of black and white and was expected to begin cleaning the house at six in the morning, serve food at large dinner parties, lived in a tiny cold garret, and had only one afternoon a week to herself. None of this apparently was as unpleasant as the attitude of the mistress of the house.

I was surprised and delighted when, after my mother had been in Englefield Green for a couple of weeks, the St. Clair postman arrived at the school one morning and brought me a small parcel from her. It contained a soft chestnut brown leather frame that displayed two brown-toned photographs. One picture was of my mother, taken about a year earlier. She wore her cream-colored woolen blouse with its wide, crocheted collar and cuffs in shades of green and smiled brilliantly into the camera, her chin resting on her hand. The large black oval onyx ring that she had always loved was prominent on her left hand. I had no idea that, as I looked upon this photograph, she was actually dressed in a harsh black frock with a lace-trimmed apron and cap. The second photograph was of myself at nine months, sitting wide-eyed on my father's lap. My father was looking confidently at the photographer and holding my small fists in hands that were at least three times as large. I took my treasure up to the bedroom I shared with Nan and Janet and placed it on my chest of drawers. There, as my mother had intended, it kept me company for the duration of my stay at the school.

From Englefield Green she moved to her next job as housekeeper/companion to Mrs. Baxendale in Tunbridge Wells. This widowed old lady lived comfortably in a spacious groundfloor flat in one of those large Victorian houses, overlooking a riotous garden, so popular in English resort towns. Every so often I was able to spend a week with my mother at her new place of employment. Mrs. Baxendale was kind and friendly. A tall and slender woman, with beautifully coiffed white hair and a large and elegant face, she made me feel at home in her harmonious rooms. For some reason, however, I did not know how to behave with my mother. She had constant duties to attend to. She was busy cleaning and poring over the old mauve cookbook, published by the school of domestic education that she had attended during the first year of her marriage and brought from Troppau. She experimented with many recipes from this book to the delight of Mrs. Baxendale, who was adventurous and enjoyed what she considered to be exotic foreign food. Later in the day my mother was expected to read to Mrs. Baxendale, to play various card games with her, and to go for walks, which I could join.

During the summer holidays, through the Reverend Daunton-Fear's connections, I had also been invited to spend a week with another wealthy widow in Tunbridge Wells so that I could be closer to my mother. Mrs. Arthur Mitchell was interested in helping Hitler refugees. For a long time I believed that "Arthur" was Mrs. Mitchell's own name, as she firmly announced herself as Mrs. Arthur Mitchell on the telephone. Mrs. Mitchell was a formidable woman whose house was filled with imposing, very dark furniture and Oriental artifacts brought back from their years of duty in India and Burma. She employed a large domestic staff, including an elderly butler who greeted me gravely when I arrived and worried about my being too noisy. I was given a large, well-appointed bedroom and expected to take somber meals alone with Mrs. Mitchell. Every morning she read prayers in her sitting room. The staff consisting of the butler, three maids, the chauffeur, and the charwoman filed in and settled on a row of chairs. When the lesson had been read by Mrs. Mitchell, everyone turned around and knelt down to pray with their elbows on the seats of their chair. I was distracted by the white bows of the aprons on the maids behinds, their thick black stockings, and the holes in the soles of their shoes, which stared me in the face as I knelt behind them.

Mrs. Mitchell had found the granddaughter of one of her friends, a little girl of my age, to play with me. One afternoon the chauffeur drove us to the movies to see *The Four Feathers*. When we came out of the cinema, we were supposed to come home by bus. The film had terrified me, and I was afraid to walk alone through the syringa-scented streets after I got off the bus. The scene in which the hero is left lying very ill in the desert, parched and blinded by the unrelenting sun, recurred in my nightmares for months. On the last day of my visit, Mrs. Mitchell presented me with a little pale green religious book of biblical excerpts. She made me promise to read *The Daily Light* every morning before breakfast. I took it back to St. Clair, where I put it in the bottom drawer of my chest and heaved a great sigh of relief at having put Tunbridge Wells behind me.

Sometime in the autumn of 1940 my mother made her last change as a domestic. Miss Stevens called me into her study and announced with a beaming face that my mother would from now on be living and working in Haywards Heath within a short walking distance of St. Clair. The new job was again that of housekeeper/companion, to a Mrs. Gold, who lived in a well-designed new house set in a delightful garden in an outlying street on the way to Lind-field. Here my mother had a lovely large bedroom with a built-in washbasin to herself and the help of a maid to clean the house. It was by far the most comfortable domestic position she had had in England so far, and it was one where I could visit her easily for a couple of hours whenever I wanted to and also stay overnight and on weekends.

I enjoyed visiting her at Mrs. Gold's much more than in Tunbridge Wells. I felt more at ease there. My mother was more at home with her duties. She had learned how to cook and now had someone else to help with the rough housework. Mrs. Gold was much younger than Mrs. Baxendale, and she and my mother seemed to enjoy each other's company.

On her free afternoons, my mother sometimes came to tea at St. Clair, where she and Miss Stevens chatted in the upstairs sitting room or the study. One of these occasions in the late autumn of 1940 was the day after I had begun to bleed. It was a relief to have Miss Stevens deal with this business in her kindly, matter-of-fact manner. During her explanation, I had a vivid memory of my mother's mysterious white box in our lavatory at home. Every so often the maids had emptied it of small bloody cotton towels, which they then washed and boiled in the laundry kettle. Miss Stevens must have relayed the news that she had explained the mechanics of menstruation and had fitted me out with the necessary equipment. As I left them in the hall and walked upstairs, I saw the two women's faces lifted upward to follow my progress. My mother's expression was sad and wistful. I was not her little girl any longer. But perhaps even more important, somehow she knew that I had grown away from her and had become more Miss Stevens's daughter and that I was comfortable with this state of affairs.

CHAPTER

5

THE YEAR 1942 WAS A
watershed. Three momentous things happened: I passed the
school certificate examination, which meant that I had to
leave St. Clair and Miss Stevens, where I had felt so wonderfully at home; the British government lifted the restriction
that forced aliens like my mother to work as domestics;
and, unbeknownst to us in England, as we had no means
of communicating, the Nazis in Prague sent all Jews to
concentration camps. My father was among them. But all
that I knew was that the concerned letters he had written
to me since we had been in England and that I carried
about with me had ceased to arrive.

Sometime late in 1941 my mother's Haywards Heath
employer, Mrs. Gold, invited her relatives Leslie and Mary
Gunn to take refuge in her home in Summerhill Lane. During the heavy night air raids, this middle-aged couple had
been bombed out of their house in Croydon, a town about
halfway between London and Haywards Heath. Leslie and
Mary Gunn and my mother quickly became good friends,
my mother still in her capacity of housekeeper/companion.

Uncle Leslie, as I soon came to call Mrs. Gold's cousin, was a large and comfortable solicitor in the City and continued to go up to London by train from Haywards Heath while they lived in Mrs. Gold's house.

Miss Stevens and the Gunns conferred on the subject of my future education. St. Clair was not large enough to include a sixth form where I might obtain the necessary preparation for a university degree. It was therefore decided that it would be best for me to spend one or two years in the sixth form of one of the famous schools of the Girls Public Day School Trust, the Croydon High School for Girls. The Gunns, who knew it well, thought that the trust might be willing to make a financial concession to me as a refugee. Consequently, I was invited by the trust committee to come to its London headquarters and prove myself suitable material for their largesse. My mother escorted me, dressed in my best hand-me-down frock, on one of the few occasions that I saw London during the war. The trust's offices were somewhere behind Hanover Square, but the classical proportions of that part of the town interested me less than the severity of the three examiners whose questions I was expected to field from the opposite side of a long rectangular table. Two gray, elderly men and a woman with a lisp quizzed me in order to discover my facility with English and my general attitude to education and to my future. I must have satisfied them as, soon afterwards, I received a letter announcing that I would be admitted to the Croydon High School for Girls at the beginning of the next school year.

At the same time that I was planning to move from Haywards Heath to the Croydon High School, my mother was allowed to look for employment that was not domestic. As millions of British office workers had volunteered or been drafted into the military services, the lack of civilian personnel now forced the government to permit "friendly" aliens to work in their place. On leaving school, as a young woman, my mother had worked as a law clerk for her father, and she now considered doing something similar. Again, Uncle Leslie was helpful and, through his legal connections, found an eminent firm in Bishopsgate in the City that offered her a position. The senior partner of this firm, Mr. Joseph, belonged to one of the renowned Jewish families in England. Later I learned that they all knew each other and were often interrelated and known as "the cousinhood." Mr. Joseph and his wife were interested in the arts and sang as the mainstays of a well-known Highgate choir. Over the next thirty years, my mother remained with this firm and soon worked her way up from a position of lowly clerk to become its main trust and tax officer in charge of large family and company trusts and holdings.

At the end of the summer term of 1942, the London bombing had somewhat abated, and though their own home was uninhabitable, the Gunns moved back to a rented house in their neighborhood in South Croydon and took my mother to stay with them. She immediately began her new job, commuting daily with Uncle Leslie from the Southern Railway hub of East Croydon station to London Bridge in the City.

Soon afterwards I also went to Croydon to be interviewed by Miss Adams, headmistress of the Croydon High School. The school consisted of a dauntingly large and somber collection of nineteenth-century redbrick buildings. Miss Adams was a small, round woman, briskly efficient and far more formidable than Miss Stevens, whom I considered a member of my family. However, she was kind and seemed to understand the strangeness I felt in these new surroundings. She was also concerned about my living arrangements. The Gunns had offered my mother a room in their house while she got settled in her new job, but they did not have space for me or the complications a teenaged girl would bring into their household. Miss Adams told me that for several years a Croydon family whose mother and three daughters were all "old girls" had harbored Nazi refugee pupils of the school. This family was eager to take another and would like to meet me.

So began my long-lasting relationship with a fascinating family, the Crags, whose charitable impulses and quirky dry sense of humor were a constant source of surprise and inspiration. The parents, Chris and Iris, owned a large three-story detached house, called Waxham, not far from where my mother now resided with the Gunns in South Croydon. Here they lived with their two youngest adopted children and a motley group of boarders. Their four natural children were fully grown and busy in the working world. But four children had not been enough for Chris and Iris, and they soon adopted others or, as in my case, took them in as foster children. I knew immediately I set foot in Chris and Iris's house that I would enjoy being with them. Iris was a spiky and somewhat prickly person, with curly white hair impervious to any attempted tidying. Almost nothing ever escaped her brilliant blue eyes, and if it did, her pointed nose quickly discovered it in some other way. She bustled about the house and the town, always organizing and nudging her family and everyone else to be more effective, whether in homework, some charitable enterprise, or simply setting the table or clearing up one's room.

Her husband, Chris, complemented her admirably. He was a tall, lean, and handsome man, with curved and bushy eyebrows. His ruddy, craggy, finely chiseled face was always in repose. Nothing discomposed him: neither German bombs, accidents, illnesses, nor the tumult caused by the ever-growing family of strangers in his household. His curiosity was as deep as Iris's, and he tried to put it to good use both for the Royal Geological Society, of which he was a fellow, and his family and friends. A dreamy man, we would come upon him washing the dishes with his long bare fingers while Iris shouted at him to use the dishrag. Every morning during these beleaguered days of scarcity, he put bicycle clips on his trousers and cycled around the neighborhood shoveling the droppings from the milkman's horse into a little box he had fastened to the back of his Raleigh. Later, he lovingly spread this "gold dust," as he called it, around the plants and fruit trees in the large garden behind the house and in his vegetable allotment in an open part of the town.

The fruit trees, particularly Chris's beautiful plum trees, were most valuable during the war, now that it was impossible to import oranges for making marmalade. Chris was the jam- and marmalade-maker in the family, and on many summer days the house smelled deliciously of the plum, blackberry, and gooseberry jams he concocted. Friends and relatives saved up the extra sugar rations provided for people who were able to put up preserves and brought them to Chris in return for receiving some of his renowned products.

Chris was a neverending source of interest and information. He and Iris were Fabians and belonged to the South London group of the Fabian society founded by Shaw, the Webbs, and H. G. Wells. He often mentioned these luminaries, who signified very little to me at that time. He still corresponded with G.B.S. and often entertained us at mealtimes by reading aloud one of the cryptic postcards he had just received from him.

Although he was undoubtedly an intellectual, lack of funds had prevented Chris from attending university, a circumstance he bitterly resented, especially as he got older. He provided a comfortable living for his large family from a fairly lowly civil service job with the custom and excise department. His daughters told the story of how he had missed the bus for the civil service examination, arriving just half an hour before the end, and still passed the exam with an outstanding 100 percent. He had a passion for geology and botany and spent a great deal of time writing papers for the Royal Geological Society and in a room at the back of the house devoted to building a regional survey model of the town of Croydon. This impressive structure depicted the town's population, natural environment, and geography with fascinating intricacy. The model room was the only place in the house that was out of bounds, except when Chris was there. Toward the end of the war, Chris became involved with Francis Butler and Professor Tansley of Cambridge in creating the Council for the Promotion of Field Studies and later was the first director of the council's center at Juniper Hall in Surrey.

One of the greatest problems during the war years, particularly in large, draughty houses like Waxham, was to keep warm. The corridors, bedrooms, and bathroom of Chris and Iris's house were uncomfortably cold, even when we had enough coal or coke to keep the living room fire alight. Chris hated the icy blasts of the unheated corridors and lavatories as much as the rest of us. And sometimes we children were intrigued to find him peeing into the scullery sink when he thought nobody was around. We girls giggled over this feat, and although we adored him, we were quite annoyed with him, both as an adult and as a man, for being able to resort to such an unfair advantage.

Chris and Iris's children were all interested in medicine. The oldest daughter, Mary, was a nurse and had joined the Queens District Nurses. Graham was a physician, specializing in pediatrics. Their second daughter, Jean, occasionally appeared at home in the smart naval uniform of a W.R.E.N. officer. The youngest of Chris and Iris's natural children, Pat, now in her late teens, was temporarily at home when I came to live with them. She had been training as a nurse at St. Bartholomew's Hospital in London and, because of the nursing shortage, was so exhausted that the doctors suspected tuberculosis. Pat therefore spent her days resting in a supposedly healthy, damp and chilly bedroom overlooking the street, and, as she was closest to me in age, we soon became good friends. She had inherited her crisply dry sense of humor from her father, and we seemed to be laughing all the time.

A couple of years younger than I, there was the adopted son, Norman, who attended the well-known local Whitgift school for boys and was a member of the school band. Early in the morning and late at night, we could hear him practicing his trumpet diligently and noisily in the bedroom across the hall. Sometimes he appeared, dressed only in a floating white shirt, trumpeting boisterously in the doorway of my room. Blue-eyed with delicate blond hair and features, Norman remains with me as a trumpeting Peter Pan rather than the banker he later became.

One of the great revelations of this household was the nonchalance with which we all piled into the bathroom. Wartime restrictions both on water and on coal made it imperative to use a minimum amount of hot water. The government suggested that five inches of bathwater were adequate, and many good citizens had a line drawn inside their bathtubs at five inches to ensure adherence to this rule. Since Chris and Iris's family was constantly increasing, and the children often visited home together with innumerable friends, the whole family shared the bathwater, several members climbing one after another into the used water, which gradually became more and more tepid. The whole scene was reminiscent of an irreverent and cheerful royal levee, with one member of the household in the tub, while others wandered in and out, sitting companionably on the rim of the tub, on a stool or a clothes hamper. The occasions when the oldest sister, Mary, brought her nursing colleagues, particularly a jolly young woman called Afra, stand out as memorably riotous. These gatherings quickly removed any inhibitions one might have had, as the family took nakedness for granted. It was a far cry from Miss Stevens's prim attitude to the body.

In the late spring of 1943, it was decided that Pat, her cousin Celia, and I should spend a week in the family cottage between Bognor Regis and Littlehampton on the Sussex coast, where in peacetime they usually passed summer holidays. Accordingly, Chris accompanied the three of us, aged seventeen to nineteen, on the train to Bognor and settled us into the cottage. Before his return to Croydon, we all sat down to a nice afternoon tea. Chris had brought a pot of his plum jam to leave with us as a special treat during our stay. We had acquired a crusty loaf of bread from the local baker and sat in happy expectation of our week of freedom from grownup supervision. Chris chatted comfortably, telling us to be sure to lock the cottage carefully when we left it and also to eat the jam as sparingly as possible or it would not last the week. As he talked he spooned larger and larger dollops of the precious jam onto his bread. We three girls could hardly contain our laughter, but Chris was quite oblivious to what he was doing. When he had finally departed, we inspected the jam jar only to find that he had left us just enough for one thinly covered slice of bread each.

Not long after we had gone to sleep on our first night in Bognor, we were awakened by the wailing of the air-raid sirens. Soon we heard and felt the noise and earth-shaking rumble of bombs. We had been told to get under solid cover in case of air raids, but the cottage had no cellar and we could not think of any good cover. Finally, one of us suggested the ironing board, so giggling helplessly at what we knew to be ridiculous, we cowered under the ironing board until the all-clear sounded and we were able to stretch out comfortably in our beds.

Despite these setbacks, we enjoyed our week at the

seaside. We had long lazy hours on the beach and made excursions to the Roman town of Chichester, where we explored the small cathedral, and to Arundel Castle. We walked along the river at Arundel, having bought a loaf of bread to take home later on. As we walked, we were increasingly overcome by such hunger pangs that we began to tear off pieces of the large loaf. Even as we did so, we told each other to remember Chris and the jam, but we did not seem to be able to prevent ourselves from devouring the fragrant bread, and so we gave up and demolished the entire loaf, sitting by the river in the shadow of the duke of Norfolk's imposing structure.

It was as we sat there enjoying the tranquility of this romantic setting that Pat began to speak of the difference between me and the other refugee girls who had been living in her parents' house before me. She wondered how I had escaped the seriousness of my predecessors. These other girls, no older than Pat or myself, had a maturity and sophistication that had left Pat and her sisters feeling childish and excluded. Pat told us how awkward she felt when these refugee girls, who were in her form at the Croydon High School or even younger, used to hold long, solemn evening conversations with her mother, Iris, while she was sent off to bed. It irked and depressed her and made her feel not a little envious. We speculated about these girls' sophistication and their experiences. Whatever the reason, Pat admitted that it was a great relief to have someone like me who was able to laugh and giggle like an ordinary girl of seventeen. I, in turn, began to wonder why I was not more serious. Was I ignoring or suppressing something of the seriousness of my situation?

When we returned to Croydon, I found that a significant letter awaited me from the education division of the exiled Czech government offices in London.

Soon after Neville Chamberlain had agreed, at Munich in September 1938, to Hitler's demands for the carving up of Czechoslovakia and the Nazi annexation of the Sudetenland, the Czech president, Edvard Beneš, had resigned. Just before Hitler marched into the Czech capital on the Ides of March of 1939, a KLM plane swooped into Prague and spirited eleven secret agents and several cases of vital government documents to London. Some seven million pounds of gold from the Czech National Bank had also been saved from Nazi rapaciousness and transported via Switzerland and the Bank of England to be used for Czech exiles and the war effort. The British government also had made a grant of four million pounds to aid Czech refugees. With the support of the British and French governments, Beneš then formed a Czech National Committee, which eventually operated in London as the Czech government in exile. Throughout the war, this Czech government in London concerned itself not only with the maintenance of a Czech army and airforce, allied to the British army and the RAF, and with political plans for the future of the republic after the war, but also with the welfare of Czech refugees in Britain. A network of Czech secret service agents worked between London and Prague from that time and throughout the six years of the war, maintaining contact between the exiled government and the Czech resistance movement.

Of vital importance both to the Nazi occupiers of Czechoslovakia and to the Czech people was the suppression of the present and future intelligentsia through the curtailing of education. All Czech universities had been closed after anti-German student demonstrations in 1939. In May of 1942 some exiled Czech army officers had flown from England and parachuted into the Czech countryside, assassinating the harsh and terrorizing German "protector" and general of police, Reinhard Heydrich. Brutal reprisals such as the razing of the Czech mining village of Lidice

FROM AN ALBUM

Troppau: Palais Sobeck in the 1930s.

Troppau: Father and daughter.

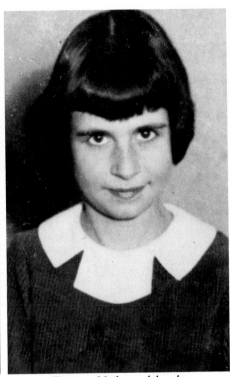

Troppau: Mother and daughter.

St. Clair's School, Sussex.

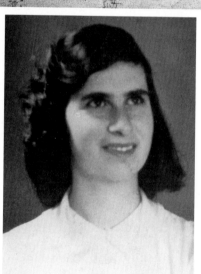

Susan, 1942.

Miss Wiltshire, Janet, Susan, Nan, 1941.

Abernant School, Wales.

From class picture: Julian, far right top row; Susan, far left, middle row.

V-E Day: Auditorium ready for celebration.

Prague , 1946: Boating on the Vltava.

Prague , 1946: Shopping, Na Příkopě.

England, 1947: Susan.

Barbara Hammond, 1948.

London: Mother in 1982, aged 82,
3 years before her death.

and the killing of two hundred of its inhabitants and the deportation to concentration camps of the remaining women and children followed. Morever, a serious crackdown on Czech secondary education took place throughout the country. "An elementary school with five classes is enough for you," Czechs were told by the new Reich protector.

The letter I received then in the summer of 1943 from the education division of the exiled Czech government in London urged, as on several previous occasions, that I should attend their free, government-sponsored boarding school, which was preparing young Czech refugees like myself to return to their homeland after the war. There we would be urgently needed to help rebuild our country that had for years been under Nazi domination with little or no secondary education. Suddenly this avenue seemed the only sensible course for my immediate future. I felt that I had reached an age and a point in my life when the Czech school sounded not only like an exciting venue, but it also offered an idealistic involvement in creating a better future for our world after the war was won. Further, I would need to know more about Czechoslovakia, where I assumed my future lay, than I could learn in my English schools.

Although I loved living in Chris and Iris's household, I was not enjoying the Croydon High School. While I had performed well in the intimate milieu of St. Clair, I felt out of my depth at the school in Croydon. The latter was very large and the number of pupils in my class seemed overwhelming. I hated the sports, particularly the compulsory games of hockey, from which I always returned home with bruised and massacred ankles. I did not even like the dances to which some of the girls in my form invited me. My academic performance suffered, and I missed Miss Stevens and her staff's comforting tutoring. Although passing the Oxford school certificate examination with several distinctions had made it possible for me to matriculate at London

University, I was not as confident of my scholastic ability at Croydon as I would have wished.

So I went to see my mother to discuss the possibility of my accepting the Czech government's proposition. She was dubious on several counts. She was not at all sure that I would feel comfortable surrounded by refugee children, since I had never been involved with refugees as long as I had been in England. Moreover, she herself was about to move in with Chris and Iris as one of their boarders and had looked forward to living under one roof with me for the first time since our leaving Czechoslovakia. However, the more I thought about this new idea, the more it appealed to me, and eventually I persuaded myself and my mother that I should complete my school years at the Czech school rather than in Croydon.

And so at the beginning of the next term I found myself with about a hundred Czech refugees at Euston Station. The train taking our school from London to Llanwrtydd Wells in Wales was crowded with children and young people, most of whom had known each other for many years. They had all been at the Czech school in Shropshire before it expanded. Now, for the remainder of the war, the Czech government in London had rented the luxurious Abernant Lake Hotel on the Breconshire moors, where it installed its "Gymnasium." Everything was financed by the government—the teachers' salaries and living expenses, as well as the students' tuition and their room and board. This school, which I was about to join, and where I remained for two years from the age of seventeen, was different from anything I had experienced before. First of all, it had a political mission that permeated all our activities; second, it was a coeducational boarding school; and third, it was situated in a luxury hotel in a beautiful scenic resort.

On that first day, when I had traveled with the others

by train from Euston, we arrived in Llanwrtydd Wells after midnight. Dead tired, we were bundled off into our allocated bedrooms. I was to sleep in a bunk bed, sharing a room with three other girls, all of us somewhere between sixteen and nineteen years old. Two of these girls, chubby round Mirka and tall dark Blanka, both eighteen, were already close friends. The third was a small blond girl with widely spaced gray eyes, a finely chiseled face, a slight upper body, and very wide hips. Her name was Hedy. She offered me a choice of beds, and for the remainder of my stay at the school she slept in the bunk above me. My greatest piece of luck in this entire enterprise was that I had been allocated to share a room with Hedy, who became my friend for life.

Once again, I had to get used to another name. I found that I was to be called Groagová, short and simple, by the teachers in class and by the other pupils, except by my closest friends. I was shy and somewhat uncomfortable with all these boys and girls who not only knew each other well, but seemed to lapse easily from English into Czech as though both languages were the same. Any Czech I had learned in my early childhood had long since evaporated, and I was forced to begin all over again. Czech, moreover, was the official language of the school. In this language all lessons, homework, games, and most extracurricular activities were conducted. It was clear that we all needed both to speak and to feel Czech, as the aim of the school was to prepare us to rebuild the republic devastated by the Nazis.

After a while I discovered that many of the pupils spoke only Czech with their parents during the vacations. Some of them knew little English and spoke it with a strong accent. For them the foreign language was English. For me, since I had spoken German as a child at home and nothing but English for the past four years, the foreign language was indubitably Czech.

The curriculum of the school was as close as we could come to any other Czech or European secondary school. It was not a classical gymnasium in that we had no Greek, though I seem to remember struggling with translating Latin into Czech. We read a fair amount of English literature with a delightful Miss MacKenzie and French with a rather elegant but severe Madame Schlesingerová. None of these subjects caused me any problems, nor did mathematics, presumably because my English schools had prepared me to the level or possibly beyond the level we had now reached. It was in the classes in Czech history and literature that I often found myself stumbling through a haze of semi-comprehension because of the paucity of my language. Even so, as my Czech improved, I have a clear memory of the nationalistic fervor of what we were taught. I also have a strong impression that of the two men, Professors Turk and Krushina, who taught these subjects, one offered an interpretation overlaid with a nice touch of irony, while the other seemed much more serious about the material he presented.

We read and listened to a great deal about innumerable battles, the machinations of princes, kings, and emperors, the infighting of religious factions, the hurling out of windows of royal counselors. Much of this was barely comprehensible at the time and has remained with me only as the kind of history that gives "History" a bad name. But we also studied the legend of Libuše (later made into an opera by the Czech composer Bedřich Smetana), the princess who married her shepherd lover, and with him founded the royal line of the Přemyslides and the Czech nation, supposedly sometime in the ninth century. We learned of the "golden reign" of Charles IV, who, in the fourteenth century, created not only many of the wonderful Gothic parts of Prague, but also the literary flowering of vernacular language, and who founded the first university in Central

Europe; we learned that the Czech reformer Jan Hus wanted to overturn the power of the Catholic church, to change religious reading and observance from Latin to the vernacular Czech, and was burnt as a heretic at the stake in 1415, a century before the Protestant Reformation was able to succeed. This liberalizing of literacy and of religion was presented to us as the beginning of notions of democracy, a tree that later branched out throughout Europe and the Western world, but was conceived from a Czech seed. We heard that in the eighteenth century the Habsburg emperor Joseph II with his Patent of Toleration improved the position of all religious sects including the Jews of Prague, and we discovered that the political democratic revolutions of 1848 that spread throughout Europe were infused with a strong pro-Czech nationalism in Bohemia.

What strikes me in retrospect is that, although we were in the midst of a war with Germany that revolutionized and deeply affected the lives of all of us in that classroom, the general tone consistently emphasized the positive picture of constructive Czech ideas rather than the century-old historic fight against German or Austrian domination of the lands and people that now formed the Czechoslovak nation.

Many of the pupils, particularly the older boys, were intensely interested in the military and political progress of the war. As we waited for the teachers to come to the first class every morning, a tense group stood around the fireplace, reading the newspapers, while they debated the latest news. They talked about Churchill, Roosevelt, Stalin, and Beneš, not to mention various generals, admirals, and military commanders, as though they were personal acquaintances. They argued passionately about how these men were handling specific military and diplomatic events.

Although we had found a hospitable haven in England, it was hard to forget Chamberlain's sellout of Czechoslovakia at Munich. There was a strong pull towards both Stalin and Roosevelt among the pupils at the school. While many of them had been forced to leave Czechoslovakia because of Nazi antisemitism, many others, both Czechs and Sudeten Germans, were not Jewish, but had left their homes because of their parents' socialist beliefs, which naturally produced Soviet sympathies. Moreover, many felt strongly that Churchill had wanted to let Russia and Germany fight it out together and had dragged his heels in helping Russia by not opening a western front soon enough. On the other hand, Tomaš Masaryk, the first Czech president, had married Charlotte Garrigue, an American music student whom he had met in Leipzig in the 1870s. I had always been intrigued by the fact that he had taken his wife's name and appended it to his so that he was known as Tomaš Garrigue Masaryk. So we also had a close connection between the Czech republic and the United States. On the twelfth of April, 1945, when the news of President Roosevelt's death was announced, the whole school mourned a personal loss.

A boy called Honza stood out as the most thoughtful of the political classroom debaters. He was funny as well as incisive, and it did not surprise me that in later years he became a well-known journalist. Another debater was Zuza F., short and round, assertively eloquent, who always joined heatedly in these arguments and discussions waving her arms about. She later became part of an international team of European interpreters.

Major celebrations commemorated every significant date in the formation and development of the Czechoslovak state. Important members of the exiled government were invited, presented formal speeches and talked with us and the teachers. On such occasions, the great hotel ballroom was transformed into a political auditorium festooned with flags of the major allies. On the anniversary of the founding of the republic in 1918, the twenty-eighth of October

1944, for example, the centerpiece on the wall behind the stage was an enormous map of Czechoslovakia with its coat of arms trailing its motto PRAVDA VITĚZI (Truth Prevails) above. On the day after Germany's unconditional surrender, on May 8, 1945, the stage was simply dressed with the Czech, British, American, and Russian flags in the shape of a magnificent V for victory.

The government representatives exhorted us to remember these great occasions and to work hard for the future of the republic. We were always prepared for these festive days by various teachers, who had rehearsed the historical details of the designated event and taught us suitable Czech poetry, music, and opera to accompany it. Smetana's and Dvořak's romantic cadences were an everpresent background to our activities, and Smetana's *Vltava* (or Moldau) is inextricably woven into my memories of the Brecon moors, among which our luxurious school/hotel was nestled, more so than as an accompaniment of the real Vltava flowing under its famous bridge in Prague.

I was constantly taken aback by the overt insistence on patriotism and the concern with national significance. I was old enough to appreciate the necessity for national cohesion among a group of young people whose country had only a short history—a history that had been brutally smashed and which we were expected to create anew. Nevertheless, after five years of an understated English attitude to such issues, I found the deliberate chauvinism at Abernant school somewhat repugnant. But I liked the students, and their enthusiasm carried me along despite my misgivings.

From that first rather intimidating night, Hedy took me under her wing. She came from the Bohemian part of the Sudetenland. Her mother tongue, like mine, was German, but she had been at the school long enough to speak and write Czech well. Her English, also, was excellent, and although her exile was due to her parents' socialism,

and mine because of my Jewish grandparents, we understood each other right from the start. I saw her as one of
the most popular people in the school, an equal favorite
with the girls, with the boys, and even with the teachers.
Hedy knew what made the school tick and instructed me
accordingly.

This was the first time since I had come to England
that I had had an opportunity to meet boys in large numbers and at close quarters. I found that my long sojourn in
my various English schools, surrounded only by girls and
women, had made me shy and unsure of how to behave
with boys. Most of the other girls at Abernant appeared to
be much more at ease with them and knew how to make
the most of their opportunities.

Both official and unofficial gatherings were riotously
enjoyed. Czechs love to sing, and weekend evenings were
filled with choral songs and folk dancing. We were able to
make good use of the lake, the tennis courts, and the other
amenities of the hotel and its beautiful surroundings. We
played volleyball both in separate and in mixed teams. We
walked endlessly around the lake, along the little mountain
streams, and out over the moors. On weekends we walked
to outlying farms, where, to our great delight during this
food-impoverished wartime, the farmers made us delicious
afternoon teas even including fresh, large brown eggs,
which they set before us softly boiled with bread and butter.

I loved the teas and the walks about the grounds and
countryside. Unlike Hedy, who became one of the most
adept at folk dancing and taught it to newcomers, I was
less enthralled by singing, dancing, or sports. Partly this
was because sports and folk dancing are foreign to my
nature, but partly it was that I did not feel particularly
Czech. The teachers were surely aware of the fact that I did
not join wholeheartedly in the psychological and political

fabric of the school, but they were polite and treated me without discrimination.

There were no restrictions against the mingling of the sexes, except in the bedrooms. But although temporary walls had been erected halfway along the hotel corridors so that the girls' bedrooms were on one side of the school and the boys' on the other, many secret trysts were successfully arranged even at night. The result of one of these was the expulsion of an audacious, beautiful older girl. No one was surprised that the boy involved was not expelled as well. Certainly, no one would have thought of complaining about the sexist double standard so blatantly demonstrated on this occasion.

The school was a bubbling cauldron of romance between its inmates, who ranged in age from eleven to twenty. All around there were constant rumors of new romantic pairings. The most glamorous male sports personalities and political leaders were connected with the most physically attractive and sophisticated girls. If the school failed to teach me much in the way of academic knowledge, because of the poverty of my Czech, it taught me a great deal about the mechanics of sexual power.

My friend Hedy was much in demand by some of the most popular boys. She could take her choice and confided in me many of her most pressing romantic problems. One day she arrived in our room with red patches of anger discoloring her usually gentle face and told me that one of the senior boys, a close friend, had asked her in so many words to be his sexual "guinea pig." Giving him short shrift, she settled for a long and tempestuous relationship with one of the other handsome senior boys, a relationship that foundered almost weekly because his political views contrasted sharply with hers.

Perhaps the most shocking and titillating romantic school affair was that of a heavy-set master, whose deep, thick voice echoed wheezily through the classrooms, and who appeared to us to be far too old—with a quiet seventeen-year-old student. We used to pass them deep in conversation in the corridors, in the dining room, and in the intervals between meals and other school activities. The news of their marriage during one of the vacations left us quite speechless.

Several of the boys paid me attentions of various kinds, which did not touch me very deeply, as my own favorite was not among them. The nicest and most useful of these was a quiet older boy whose name was Felix. Felix made a bargain with me that in return for letting him use my bicycle whenever I didn't need it (he had none of his own), he would keep it in good order. In this respect I became the envy of the school, as Felix was a perfectionist and my bicycle ran more smoothly and shone with more sparkle than any other in Breconshire. Behind the hotel was a small redbrick cottage where we kept our dirty outdoor shoes and Wellington boots, our sports equipment, and also our bicycles. Here Felix was to be found for hours on end, polishing my bike, blowing up the tires, and doing whatever one does to keep bicycles well cared for. Occasionally, Felix and I wandered off into the countryside silently enjoying its beauty. Once, at a later date, we even had tea in London.

At different times, a couple of other boys sent me the usual Abernant love notes during the homework period, which began at eight o'clock in the evening. It was then that the whole student body assembled in the large hotel ballroom pondering over essays and mathematics till eleven at night. One or two of the staff members sat on the stage and occasionally moved around the room overseeing, what the British call "invigilating." Halfway through this long homework period, a student "service team" passed around milk and sandwiches. The service team were the love note carriers, a position of immense confidential responsibility. The love notes had to be slipped unobtrusively to their recipients, and it was not easy to escape the eagle eyes of the invigilators.

Love notes addressed to me included photographs of their authors and entreaties to meet them at the cottage where we changed our outdoor shoes or behind the boat-house at the lake or simply to dance with them at the next student dance. None of these admirers managed to produce a real spark of response in me, though I thought one of the taller ones, Miloš, rather handsome, and I enjoyed danc-ing with him. The problem was that we had nothing to talk about. Still, I was glad that I was not left out of this major underground activity of Abernant life, even though my own preference was largely unsatisfied.

I became aware of Julian as we sat in our first session in that corner classroom overlooking the lush grounds of Aber-nant Lake Hotel. We were asked, in alphabetical order, to give our date and place of birth. By now I had learned that only Czech place-names would be used, and Troppau, the unacceptable German name of my hometown, was to be wiped off the face of maps. So, echoing the boy who answered just before me, I also called out "Opava." I was greatly surprised to find anyone else coming from this small provincial town in the Sudetenland. Later I discovered that Julian was only born there, as the medical clinic in which I had also been born—and where, at the tender age of seven, my appendix had been removed—had a great reputa-tion so that doctors sent their patients to it from a large radius. Julian's real home was on my father's home ground of Ostrau, or as the Czechs called it: Ostrava.

All of this gave me an immediate interest in this young man. But what really intrigued me, as I got to know him better, was his wit and facility with English. As neither of his parents had been able to escape with him, he had spent the time before coming to the Czech school with an English family in the Lake District and was as comfortable with the language and customs as was I. Julian was dark-haired and brown-eyed and had a debonair face and manner. He was barely my height, but contrary to the need for a man to be "tall, dark, and handsome," this did not prevent me from being enchanted by him almost at once.

Julian was something of an outsider. Like me, he was not good at sports, and there was no question of his being on any of "the teams." Nor was he as overly excited about the military progress of the war, though he understood the political implications of both military and diplomatic events as well as any of the early-morning orators. While they had their heated arguments before the first morning class, he usually sat hunched over his homework, which he had neglected in favor of some more interesting reading the night before. On several occasions I was able to let him copy my algebra to speed his hurried preclass catching up. But in the midst of this scribbling, his opinion was often sought after by the political debaters, who demanded that he clarify a point or settle an argument. This he did with the least possible fuss or elaboration and then returned to his homework.

One of the most important debates in our classroom during the spring of 1945, while the Allied forces were advancing on Germany from both east and west, was how, after the war, the central part of Europe would be divided— whether the 1918 divisions would stand, or whether parts of the Third Reich should be reapportioned to some of the countries that had suffered most in the devastation. Czecho-slovakia being right in the middle of the Continent, our classroom politicians were almost as involved with the possi-bilities as the three major players at the Yalta Conference in February of 1945. Their various political allegiances were well represented in the debates, and it didn't need a particularly subtle ear to work out who was sympathetic to the Stalinist, Churchillian, or Rooseveltian point of view. Julian played his cards close to his chest, and his occasional arbitration of the debaters' deadlock appeared to me, at this time, to be based on logic and expediency, rather than on ideological premises.

After a while, Julian and I began to find each other as we went about our business in the school and that universal rendezvous, the shoe cottage. There was never any question of a prearranged tryst. If we happened to meet at a convenient time, we would walk around the lake or along the small river. If the weather was warm enough, we might sit by the bend of the river overlooking my favorite place, where the shallow weir brought the water tumbling and cascading over the rocks. Julian talked eloquently about everything that came into his head: the school, the state of the world and the war, the English family that nurtured him in Ambleside, his ideas about the future. He let me know that he enjoyed my company and our conversations. I longed for more, but he made no romantic moves, and I was far too shy and well brought up to know how to go about initiating anything of the sort myself. During our walks we often met other students and some of the teachers, who greeted us knowingly, suggesting that we were indeed a "pair." I basked in the thought that they should believe this, and in the pleasure of his company, and daydreamed about him off and on throughout my waking moments.

During a winter vacation, when the "doodlebug" bombs were particularly vicious in the London area, my mother arranged for me to stay in Manchester with my Viennese cousin, Hilde, instead of returning to Croydon. Julian traveled by the same train on his way farther north to the Lake District. We were the only two from the school to go on this train, which like all wartime trains was crammed full of passengers—old and young, soldiers and civilians, sitting tightly packed in the compartments and standing in the corridors. It was always difficult to move about on a train during the war, and having found a seat, no one would leave it for any reason whatsoever.

Sitting there, side by side in the red-and-green plush upholstered compartment, my senses were stirred by finding myself in such close proximity to Julian, accompanied by the throbbing of the train's engine. His thigh was wedged against mine by the pressure of the extra passengers who had crowded into the seats. It was a great effort not to reach out for his hand, as I felt my body flooded by one rush of love after another. I was convinced that what I felt must be reciprocated. It did not occur to me that my passionate desire might not have been shared, particularly as we had spent so many delightful times together in the Welsh countryside. But Julian seemed totally unconcerned by our position and chatted in his usual animated way about the holidays to come, asking what I would be doing, and describing the family with whom he was to spend his time in Ambleside. He lifted out my black lacquer suitcase and waved a cheerful goodbye when I descended at Manchester.

After that vacation, we reassembled at Abernant and took up our studies and friendships where we had left off. One late afternoon during the winter term, when it was already dark, I went to our classroom to fetch a book I had forgotten in my desk. I walked dreamily along to the end of the corridor, thinking how nice it would be if Julian were to be there by coincidence. As I pushed open the door and switched on the light, my heart stopped. Julian was indeed in the room. But he was not alone. Helena, one of the girls of the year below us, was also there. They stood close together by the fireplace, their faces flushed, Helena's blouse unbuttoned and her thick dark brown hair hanging disheveled around her shoulders. None of us spoke a word. I went to my desk, pulled out the book, and stumbled out of the room as fast as I decently could.

After this, my walks with Julian continued as before, but it became clear that, however much I longed for more than walks, that part of Julian's life was reserved for someone else. Even worse, I often saw him go off with Helena to the moors equipped with rugs and thermos flasks and had to pretend to others that I was unconcerned about this state of affairs. Inside, I was sick with jealousy, often preferring not to go out at all in case I met them together somewhere about the grounds.

I was sure that Julian was aware of my feelings, though he pretended to ignore them. He was somewhat apologetic when we were together, yet he appeared to make an effort to spend even more time with me. And so, while it was a bittersweet and sometimes painful situation, our friendship continued and deepened throughout our stay at Abernant and beyond.

We watched the development of the war with ever-mounting excitement. The Normandy invasion by American troops in June 1944 was a major landmark—we were sure that as of now everything would roll along smoothly. The Russian liberation of Ruthenian Carpathia, the eastern tail of the Czechoslovak fish, in October of the same year brought yet more jubilant celebrations to our flag-bedecked ballroom. And finally came the German surrender and VE day on May 8, 1945. The romantic cadences of the national anthem, "Where Is My Home," aching with longing for Bohemian and Slovak streams and mountains, flooded the building more than ever.

Immediately, we were told that the Czech government in London was making arrangements for those of us who wanted to return to Czechoslovakia to do so. The government would continue to support us while we were students;

the famous Charles University in Prague, soon to be re-opened, beckoned intriguingly. My favorite Tante Grete had studied there, as had my mother's younger brother, Uncle Fritz. The plight of the country, bereft of any second-ary schools or universities for the past few years, made our return very desirable to the republic as we had had the benefit of both English and Czech education throughout the war. Having been exposed to the idealistic atmosphere of the school, and inspired by my friends, I was determined to join the large group that planned to fly together in order to help rebuild the country.

Although aware of the obvious progress of the war, I had no idea of the complex political problems that beset the exiled Czech government in London throughout the past few years. Two major difficulties had our president, Edvard Beneš, balanced on a political tightrope. The first of these was the Czech relationship with the Soviet Union; the second was the problem of what to do about the Sude-ten Germans after the war was won.

When, at the beginning of the war, Stalin and Hitler had made a nonaggression pact, it left the Western Allies of France, Great Britain, and those exiles whom they har-bored from Nazi-dominated countries like Czechoslovakia, to fight alone. Thus it was not too surprising that the West-ern Allies were not overeager to start a second front to help Russia before they had made adequate plans and prepara-tions. But while President Beneš and Jan Masaryk, the son of the former president, had fled to London, several other prominent Czech politicians, and particularly those with communist leanings, had sought asylum in Russia. These Czech refugees to the East were later to have ever-increasing power in their own country. As the war progressed, and the major Allied leaders began to plan the future of Europe, it became clear that while American and British forces would invade Germany from the West, Russian armies would push into German-controlled lands like Poland, Hungary, and Czechoslovakia from the East. Although not a communist, Beneš had always been pro-Russian and had insisted that in due course events would force Russia against Hitler and onto the Allied side. The Nazi invasion of the Soviet Union in June 1941 proved him right, and in the midst of the war Beneš twice flew back and forth between England and Russia to mend his fences and to confer with Stalin and exiled Czechs in Moscow. His critics felt that he had shown weakness by not preventing Soviet forces and exiled Czech communists from taking the major part in the invasion and rehabilitation of Czechoslovakia at the end of the war. Yet Beneš was in no position to argue when even Churchill and Roosevelt had to defer to Stalin's demands in this matter at the Big Three conferences at Teheran in 1943, and in February of 1945 at Yalta, when Roosevelt was already mortally ill. Thus the course of communist domination of Czechoslovakia after the war was set quite early on, while none of us were aware of what was happening behind the scenes.

Beneš's problem with the future of the Sudetenland and Sudeten Germans was equally thorny. From the very beginning of the formation of the exiled Czech government, intense discussions between British, Czech, and other Allied leaders took place in London with socialist and communist refugees from the Sudetenland. The issue was simply this: should the Sudetenland be ceded to Germany as most of its people wished, or should the Sudeten Germans be evicted and leave their land to the Czechs as part of the Czechoslovak republic. As the war progressed and the Sudeten Germans in Czechoslovakia, with the backing of Hitler and his police general Heydrich, behaved ever more insolently and cruelly towards the Czechs, it became clear that the only tolerable solution of the Sudeten German problem would be their eviction.

Both of these political problems—the Russian, rather than American, British, or French liberation of Czechoslovakia, and the eviction of the Sudeten Germans—were to have significant implications for my future, but at this juncture I was unaware of them, and even had I understood would probably have been unable to relate them to my own situation. My mother, also, was not particularly astute politically, and, although clearly uneasy, she could not convincingly articulate her doubts about my youthful idealistic zeal and the irresistible pull of adventure. Moreover, we did not know what had happened to my father, and she was deeply worried about what I would find out when I began to look for him. She was very unhappy about my leaving, but despite the fact that I was still (and remained) afraid of her disapproval, my determination and enthusiasm overrode all objections. So, in late August of 1945, together with most of my intrepid friends, I boarded the American liberator bomber that safely carried me to Prague and the shock of disillusionment.

PART III

RETURN TO CZECHOSLOVAKIA

CHAPTER

6

In AUGUST OF 1945, only three months after Hitler's war had ended, I was walking about the beautiful but neglected city of Prague.

Our refugee lives in England had varied considerably, some of us having fared much better than others. For my part, everybody had been kind and generous, and the years of war spent with English children, teachers, and volunteer foster-parents had made me feel very much at home. Obviously, we suffered hardships, shortages, and deprivations such as being far from our real homes, without one or both of our parents, food rationing, and having to wear hand-me-down clothes, not forgetting the occasional near miss of a bomb or a stricken airplane hurtling from the sky. There was, however, a great feeling of solidarity, and I was never forced to think of myself as an unwanted outsider. England had indeed been a refuge and a haven.

Our return to Czechoslovakia, on the other hand, and our arrival in Prague proved a rude awakening. While waiting to get in touch with friends or relatives who would help to organize our future plans, we spent our first night in the Prague Y.M.C.A. There we slept on the floor amid rows and rows of men and women who had also arrived that very day, not like ourselves from a somewhat cossetted existence in England, but after being released from concentration camps. They were ill, weak with pain and hunger, unwashed, and psychologically remote. We felt overdressed, overfed, and ashamed of our relatively privileged condition. The pain and discomfort of that first night in Prague were deeply disturbing.

Before I left England for Prague, my mother had gently and carefully prepared me for the possibility that my father would not have survived. When she told me this, as we were lying in bed in her room one morning, I was unwilling to accept such a reality. Now, in Prague, where all my returning companions were dealing with similar traumas, I too went to the Red Cross offices where information about missing persons would be obtained. As I try to remember this occasion, I find that my mind is a complete blank. I remember many important, and far less important, moments of my life with crystal clarity, but the circumstance of this brutal revelation is as though it had never taken place. It is rather as if some skillful physician (possibly nature herself) had injected me with a strong anesthetic so that I awoke from the operation to a dull ache that remained with me for the time I stayed in Prague, and indeed for the rest of my life.

I learned some of the circumstances of my father's last years from my childhood friend Hanni, with whom I had spent much of my first twelve years in Troppau. She, and her whole family, had recently also returned to Prague from the concentration camp Theresienstadt, where they had seen something of my father. Theresienstadt (or Terezin) was not an extermination camp, and it housed mostly Czech citizens. The camp had a hospital where Hanni's mother, Tante Boeszi, had a menial job of some kind. She told me that my father had died of pneumonia in the hospital soon after he arrived there. I feared that perhaps she was telling me a comforting white lie, but was too cowardly to delve deeper.

I wandered around this ancient city, surely one of the most beautiful I have ever known, unable to cry, feeling confused and empty. I went to the last known address where my father had lived. It was a house on Mezibranska, the street leading to the National Museum and Wenceslas Square, in the center of the new town. Total strangers opened the door. They knew nothing of my father or of people who might have occupied this house in the early years of the war. I realized that my father had walked along the very pavements that were now under my feet and shied away from imagining how he must have felt during these last years of his life—left alone in a strange city. I thought of the warm and comforting letters he had written me for a few months after we left him behind, which stopped abruptly with the outbreak of war. I remembered how, full of optimism, he expected to join us soon in England; I thought of the selfless concern for my welfare that had suffused these letters written at a time when his own situation was in truth so utterly bleak. When I received them, aged thirteen, and did not yet know how this story would end, I had not felt particularly distressed at the ever more urgent concluding sentences telling me how much he missed me. But for most of my life, since I was sixteen years old and began to wonder whether I would ever see him again, I have not been able to bring myself to re-read these sad and stoic letters.

After that first night in the Prague Y.M.C.A., my friend Hedy, with whom I had returned from England, invited me to live with her. Before the war, Hedy's brother had rented a tiny apartment in the suburbs of Prague, which he was able to recover after his stint of fighting with the Jugo-slav partisans when the war was won. The apartment con-sisted of one room that housed a large bed, a kitchen stove, and a table, as well as an infinitesimally small bathroom. Hedy slept in the middle of the bed, I on one side of her, and her father, just returned from the concentration camp of Flossenburg (where he had been incarcerated for his com-munist beliefs), on the other. In comparison to the food available in Prague at this time, English wartime rationing seemed like gourmet feasts. The milk, particularly, was noticeably thin and blue. There was no coal, and as soon as the weather turned colder, we spent much of our time in this room, even in the daytime, lying in bed in our overcoats.

After a few weeks, Hedy's mother also returned from England, and she and Hedy's father went to the Giant Mountains in northern Bohemia to live in the house they had built themselves, which had been returned to them after the war. Hedy and I stayed on in the little apartment. It suddenly seemed reassuringly spacious, especially after we had exchanged the large bed for a couple of bunks in which we slept for the year during which I remained in Prague.

We now began to organize our future. Most of us who had been in the Czech school in Wales quickly completed our Czech secondary school studies by attending one of the Prague schools and after three months took a general oral "matura" examination, which ensured our entry to the uni-versity. The only part of this examination that stands out in my memory, probably because I still remember my intense surprise at knowing the answer, is a question I was asked about vectors and scalars during a grueling hour of physics. We were now, so to speak, ready for the next step of our higher education.

For Hedy this was fairly simple. She was happy to be back and reunited with her whole family, and she had long determined to become an architect. She enrolled immediately in the architecture curriculum at Charles University, the University of Prague, named for its founder, the fourteenth-century Emperor Charles IV.

For me the prospect was not so clear. In the first place, my family—aunts, uncles, and cousins—appeared to have been completely wiped out. But also, the Czechoslovakia to which I had returned was a strange and unsympathetic place, and not only because the absence of my family had robbed the country of an atmosphere recognizable as "home." It took a while for me to understand why it was so uncongenial to me, whereas some of my other returning friends, like Hedy, were reasonably content. It was not simply that I had become somewhat Anglicized and had felt truly at home among the English, although this had indeed happened. For example, I had become used to eschewing discussions of religion and politics unless I knew someone very well indeed. Yet these were the topics that formed the introduction to any conversation among strangers in this country.

More important was the fact that it gradually became clear to me that as a German-speaking Czechoslovak citizen, who had been born in the Sudetenland, I was persona non grata. I suppose I should have realized this sooner, but as we were completely accepted as Czech citizens in England, and as the teachers, administrators, and students did not discriminate against me in the Czech school in Wales, it did not occur to me that people who had been under brutal German domination for six years would not readily distinguish between Sudeten Germans expelled by the Nazis and those who had collaborated with them.

I had been too sheltered in England to be aware of the fact that the age-old enmity between Sudeten Germans and Czechs had risen to the surface with a vengeance throughout the war, brought to a high point after the assassination of the Nazi police chief Heydrich in 1942, and escalated again in the months before the final collapse of the Third Reich, when the Russian army was advancing from the East. With Hitler's ideology and S.S. troops to back them, some Sudeten Germans, like dying sharks, had behaved with reckless cruelty towards the Czechs. After their liberation, Czech nationals were unlikely to feel kindly toward anyone who spoke German or who had any German connection.

My situation became strikingly apparent to me when I tried to obtain a small part-time job in an office as a translator. I was required to fill in a form asking how my father had described himself in the national census of 1930. There were four possible answers—Czech, Slovak, German, Jewish. I did not hesitate to answer truthfully: "German." Doors immediately shut in my face. The friend from the Czech school in Wales, whose uncle had made the possibility of this job available to me, was horrified that I could have answered so naively. But it had not occurred to me to lie, and in any case I thought of myself as neither Czech nor Jewish. Neither, of course, did I think of myself as German, but it was my father's statement on the census form of 1930 that was at issue. It was this occasion in Prague that first made me aware of my place in a national, ethnic, and religious limbo, a realization that six years of gentle, and not so gentle, English jokes and nudgings about "bloody foreigners" had never achieved.

The early Czechoslovak republic, founded after the First World War, had, like Switzerland, prided itself on the peaceful coexistence of several ethnic groups. In fact, my father's abominable Czech caused several Czech judges, before whose courts he appeared as an attorney throughout the 1920s and 1930s, to beg him to continue his discussion in German. "For God's sake, Herr Doktor, speak German," they would say. My Czech, despite a Czech governess in my childhood and almost two years of compulsory Czech essay writing and class discussions in the school in Wales, was as abominable as my father's. The only difference was that I now spoke it with an English accent.

Apart from the problem of not being "a real Czech," I was also neither a real Jew nor a communist. Either of these solid identities would have given me an acceptable entree and a sense of belonging to Czech society in the years immediately after the country regained its autonomy. While all four of my grandparents had been Jews, my parents had abandoned the faith and become as assimilated as possible. When I was born, I was christened and, as a child, attended the Lutheran Sunday school. Although by the time I arrived in Prague in 1945, God and religion seemed irrelevant to my life, I had taken part in Anglican church services at my English schools and had, after a great deal of wrangling with the instructing vicar, been confirmed by the bishop of Chichester. Moreover, I had never considered Judaism as a racial quality—that was something Hitler had foisted on us, and Hitler's laws were surely null and void. As far as I was concerned, Judaism was a religion that I had practiced neither as a child nor later.

At one point during the early part of my stay in Prague, various friends urged me to look for financial assistance from the Jewish relief fund for returning refugees. When I wrote to my mother in London of this suggestion, she was incensed that I should even consider such a course. To her strict sense of integrity, this would be totally inadmissible. She and my father had abandoned the Jewish faith; I had never been part of it; it would be taking money under false pretenses; we had forfeited the right to accept such moneys. In vain did other Jewish friends, and even administrators of the relief fund, argue that as my father had been forced to die in a concentration camp and as I had lost my home because of my Jewish ancestry, I was surely eligible for assistance from Jewish sources. They even reasoned that it was my parents and not I who had made the decision to abandon Judaism and that I should not therefore suffer a double persecution now. But my mother was adamant. She declared that she would send me some of her meager salary until I found a job, and I followed her wishes. In retrospect I believe that her decision was admirable and correct.

As for communism, which now offered many Czechs and returning exiles a secure road to a future, this was not my style. I appreciated socialist ideals of internationalism against narrow chauvinism. I believed also, and still do, in the importance of a system of nationalized, egalitarian, and free education and health care as it is obviously wrong for individuals who are weak, either because of their youth or the failure of their bodies, to have to provide for their own welfare. And I was pleased to be directly involved in such planning later on in England, when a Labour Government carried out its welfare state program. But there was something in the political drive and also the secrecy of the communist wave that swept Czechoslovakia at that time that I found extremely uncomfortable, not to say offensive, to the core of my being. Yet I was happy and relaxed in the company of my closest communist friends who had returned with me from England, which only goes to show that either they did not know what they were letting themselves in for or that close knowledge of individuals blinds one to the inhumaneness of totalitarian movements.

In any case, I was incapable of adhering either physically or spiritually to a Czech, a Jewish, or a communist group. This meant that I was probably one of a tiny number of returning refugees who had no community ready to provide financial aid of any sort.

I pondered the disturbing nature of my position—of belonging and yet not belonging—and finally realized that my romantic notions of helping to rebuild this beautiful but shattered country were unrealistic. I decided that I would eventually have to return to England, where I had felt much more at home than I now did in the land of my birth. Instead of registering at the university (which would also have assured me financial assistance) like most of my returning friends, I therefore began to apply for an English visa and, while waiting, looked for a job to keep me fed.

My first attempt with a Czech firm having failed because of my "German" ancestry, I thought it would be easier to find a place among foreign employers. Luckily, the British Council, an organization loosely attached to the British government as a worldwide cultural information bureau, offered me employment in their library, to work on translations and correspondence. It was not a particularly fascinating job, but it served until I could get back to England. And the people around me were pleasant and kind. Connected to the British Council was the British Institute, whose director at this time was the Scottish poet Edwin Muir, a lecturer on English literature and intellectual history at Charles University. Muir was a shy and introverted presence in the background of these splendid British Council offices in Panska Street housed in a baroque palace with a magnificent staircase. As the translators of Kafka, he and his wife, Willa, knew Prague from their earlier stay in the 1920s. In his *Autobiography* Muir described the Prague he found on his return in August 1945. He too was stunned by the change that had come over the country, not merely the physical change, but even more the psychological change among its people.

There now followed a long period of attempting to obtain the visa permitting my return to London. The British consulate insisted that I had been repatriated and that I now belonged to Czechoslovakia as a Czech citizen. I realized that my psychological feelings of "not belonging" would cut no ice with consular authorities and argued rather that, as a minor, my place was with my only living parent, my mother, residing in London and soon to become a British subject. For a year this wrangle continued. I paid weekly visits to the British consulate, where I sat in the outer office discussing my need for a visa with the most junior Czech employee, never able to reach the eyes or ears of even a medium-level English official.

These visits were interspersed with my work at the British Council and a fair amount of pleasure in the delights that Prague still had to offer. The architectural impact of the Old Town was very moving, as was the Charles Bridge over the Vltava leading to "Mala Strana" (the Lesser Town) and the ancient castle and cathedral on the hill. My innate love of exhilarating architecture was enhanced by my years at the Czech school in Wales, where art historical lectures had ensured my appreciation of these particular treasures. Many of the wonderful town squares, edged with innumerable churches and splendid baroque palaces, I saw for the first time with friends who had returned with me from Wales. A constant companion was Julian, who like myself was a newcomer to the beauty of Prague as he also had been raised in the provinces.

Throughout the year, I was comforted not only by friends who had been in England with me but also by various other old friends who were then living in Prague. First and foremost was my childhood companion, Hanni Nath, who had spent the war years in Theresienstadt with her sister and parents. All four of them had survived this brutal experience and had now been given a choice of good Prague apartments abandoned by Germans who had fled before the liberating Russian armies. In the concentration camp, Hanni had fallen in love with Jirka, a young expert on musical instruments from Prague. Toward the end of the war, he was suddenly transferred to Auschwitz, but by some miraculous combination of unusual Nazi inefficiency and quick-wittedness on his part, he managed to escape from this terrible camp. As soon as the Allies entered Czechoslovakia, he made his way back to Theresienstadt to find Hanni. After they returned to Prague, Hanni and Jirka were married. Her younger sister, Vera, fired with romantic idealism, was on the point of emigrating to Palestine and encouraging the whole family to do the same. Hanni, her husband, and parents welcomed me often to their homes. Her mother, whom I still called Tante Boeszi, made a living by sewing. She fabricated some elegant dresses and blouses for me out of creamy parachute silk that American and British airmen were selling stealthily. It was a long way from the shimmering bolts of cloth Hanni's father and uncle had sold in their exotic shop in Troppau, but the familiar ambience was still there.

Another friendly Prague apartment was the hiding place of my favorite Tante Grete's former husband, Bruno. Bruno, who had been the correspondent of the prewar and internationally respected German-language newspaper *Prager Tagblatt*, and continued to work for this newspaper throughout the war, was now a victim of reverse ethnic persecution and forced to leave Prague and find refuge in Germany. He never left his apartment as he would have to walk the streets wearing a white armband, advertising his racial German background.

The problem of the Sudeten Germans and all German residents in Czechoslovakia that had preoccupied the Czech government and some Allied discussions during the war was finally to be solved by an internationally controlled transfer of the Sudeten Germans to Germany and Austria. It had become clear that most Sudeten Germans were unable to coexist peaceably under Czech rule and their behavior during the Nazi period could be neither forgotten nor forgiven.

During the months immediately following the end of

the war, some brutal Czech reprisals against Germans in Czechoslovakia and particularly in the Sudetenland took place. Descriptions of these even found their way into the British and American press. There was some looting of German homes and shops. Sudeten Germans were treated similarly to Jews under the Nazis. They were forced to wear white armbands in public, had smaller food rations than the Czechs, and were taken to concentration camps. After August 1945, somewhat more humane rules were laid down jointly by the new Czech government and the International Control Commission. It was agreed that those Germans who could prove that they had been loyal to the republic were to be given Czech citizenship and could remain if they wished. But about two and a half million Germans in the new republic were to be transferred out of the country without families being separated. They should be transported in well-heated trains and allowed to take their personal belongings and one thousand Reichsmarks. American observers agreed that, although such a transfer could hardly take place without much personal hardship, it was being carried out as humanely as possible under the circumstances. And during the time that I was in Czechoslovakia, about one and a half million Germans were transferred in this organized movement to the American-controlled zone.

Bruno and his sister, Hilde, who had been my embroidery teacher in elementary school, were being hidden and supported by Bruno's Czech lover, Lydia, until they could safely leave Prague. All three shared a tiny flat in the center of the town, with Lydia, the possessor of a well-paying job, going about gathering news and scrounging for food. She seemed to have splendid connections among peasants, who supplied her with luxuries such as butter, goose liver, chickens, and as much pork and fruit as they could eat. But perhaps the most comforting part of Bruno's and Lydia's flat was its modern bathroom with unlimited hot water. As the bathwater in the flat I shared with Hedy had to be heated with coke, which was almost unobtainable, I went to Bruno's apartment at least once or twice a week to have a luxurious, and warming, bath and often took Hedy with me.

Bruno, and particularly Hilde, were terrified of leaving the flat, so they enjoyed all the company they could get. He was a fascinating and witty man, and we had many pleasant hours enjoying our conversations, the baths, and Lydia's mouthwatering food. It was she who later found me special care packages to take to hungry friends in Vienna and Paris. At one point during the year, when Tante Grete arrived from London, we all had a wonderful reunion; her divorce from Bruno had been a civilized affair, and their friendship endured. Before Bruno finally left the country, he gave me one of his treasured, splendidly illustrated volumes describing the magnificent architecture of Prague.

Occasionally, I also traveled in other parts of the country. Nostalgically, I visited my former hometown of Troppau, now known only by its Czech name: Opava. The town had been in the direct firing line of the advancing Russian army. Official reports claimed that 60 percent of the town was destroyed and lay in ruins when I saw it. Even so, much that I knew was still there, although true to form, everything seemed very much smaller than I had remembered: my old school playground, the town park, the town center, the museum that used to be under the direction of one of my father's friends, Dr. Braun. The main department store, Breda and Weinstein, previously owned by one of my mother's earliest admirers, Robert Weinstein, was practically empty and now had none of the tempting goods that once made it a Christmastime fairyland. The coffeehouses in the town park, where, on summer afternoons, my mother had danced in her elegant silk dresses, were deserted. I stood in front of the badly damaged theater, renowned for its classical façade, remembering my parents' story of how once, in the early thirties, they were enjoying a performance of *Lady Windermere's Fan* on this very stage. Suddenly they realized to their horror that her ladyship was sitting on a leather armchair belonging to our drawing room furniture, which they had imagined to be safely in storage during a removal from one house to another.

While in Troppau, I stayed with our old friend Tante Elsa, who had taught me a little English during those fraught months before my mother and I departed from the town. She had survived the holocaust by hiding in Hungary and had now returned to her architect husband, an Aryan, and the comfortable house he had designed for them, the house to which, seven years previously, I had walked through the town park fearing the harassment of boys who wanted me out of their school and out of their lives. Because of her Jewishness Tante Elsa was now able to protect her husband, a non-Jewish Sudeten-German, from the prevailing anti-German treatment by revengeful Czechs.

One afternoon during my stay, I visited my dear Tante Grete's sister, Alice, a dentist, whom as a child I had known only slightly. Looking pale and ravaged, Alice had recently returned from the concentration camp in Theresienstadt and was now reunited with her Aryan Czech husband. She was very ill with thrombosis and sat in a darkened room with her leg propped up on a cushion. After we had some tea and rather desultory conversation, Alice suddenly asked her husband to bring her a small wooden box. She opened it carefully and presented me with its contents. What I held in my trembling hand was my father's silver pocket watch, which he had given her for safekeeping. As my fingers closed around its curved rim, I finally understood the reality of my loss, and, for the first time since I had become aware of the disaster that had befallen us, I was overcome by tears.

*   *   *

During my rediscovery of Troppau, I wandered about the town past the garden of my old piano teacher and relived some of my childish terror of lurking danger in its bushes, when I was forced to find my way to and from her house on dark winter afternoons. I looked at the remaining churches and meditated on the religious instruction of my childhood. I remembered the official lessons from the Lutheran minister; how I had often accompanied the Catholic maids to their devotions; the genuine belief of our maid, Martha, who had practiced Christian charity by not deserting us after the Nazi takeover; and the catastrophes that came upon my family and Jewish friends. I realized that my childhood religion had been no more to me than my music lessons, a way of becoming acquainted with a subject, whose meaning I would later have to evaluate. I knew now that, although I would never be a performing musician, my piano lessons, together with the concerts I had heard, had promoted a love for sound that was unlikely to leave me. Yet neither my religious instruction nor later attendance at church had succeeded in fostering any faith. The best my youthful religious upbringing had achieved was a puzzled interest in the fact that so many millions could adhere to cultural and religious ideas that brought so few, if any, benefits; but it had also left me with a deep appreciation of the aesthetic qualities of fine churches and religious services.

Miraculously, the beautiful street where we had lived had survived the last-ditch Nazi defense against the Russian army. Our old home, the Palais Sobeck-Skal, was being turned into a museum and archive. As I stood there overwhelmed by poignant memories, looking up at the generous windows of our drawing room and my bedroom, I realized that my old world had gone beyond recall. Not only had many of the people who moved about these rooms during my childhood physically disappeared from the face of the earth; but also their view of life, their customs and manners, and their understanding of what life was all about were no longer recognizable. But it was not merely that the old world had vanished. I too had changed so that I could no longer imagine myself living in this house in the shadow of my mother's leisurely days, surrounded by the maids and teachers who had created my existence before I was twelve. And on some deeper level I also realized that I alone was responsible for my present predicament. I would have to find a way out of it; my parents could no longer make decisions for me.

Right on cue, as I was trying the ancient curved brass handle of the great portal of our old house, a voice behind me called my name. It was the husband of the governess who had tried to teach me to speak Czech. Remarkably, he happened to be passing at that very moment and had recognized my back, although in the intervening seven years I had changed from a child into a young woman. He invited me to come and see them, and we had a sad, but warm conversation. They had survived the Nazi terror and as Czechs were only too relieved that the previous six years were finally behind them. I asked about the Sobeck-Skals. The baron, they told me, was incarcerated in a house on the other side of the town park. Incarcerated? Yes, indeed. The Germans left in this part of the Sudetenland were being herded up and would be evicted from the country.

I went to see the baron. While waiting to be deported to Austria, he was spending his time sorting out old documents belonging to the town. He was working under the supervision of some Czech guards. He wore the obligatory white armband. We were both embarrassed. I asked about the furniture he had stored for us. He replied that he last saw our brown leather sofa and armchairs in one of his fields. Soldiers of the Red Army were comfortably ensconced in them—milking his cows. I asked about his nephew, Bubi, with whom I had played so many boisterous games. He had been killed fighting for the Germans in Russia. I asked about the baroness. "Ah," he answered, "Ina has been in Vienna for two years. She is in her apartment."

I pondered the baron's answer as we stood there among the dusty papers. Obviously the baroness had understood that once the German Reich had been defeated, Czechoslovakia would expel all Sudeten Germans, especially aristocrats such as herself and the baron, who owned large landed estates. Moreover, her aristocratic Russian ancestry was hardly likely to endear her to the Soviet forces who liberated Troppau from the east. She had carefully removed herself to Vienna in good time. Her apartment there had offered an appealing and convenient refuge to her, as it had to my mother and me in 1939. When later I spent a week in Vienna, I was unable to see the baroness there, but I heard that she supported herself by selling tickets in the box office of a Viennese theater. This was a far cry from the exotic figure always accompanied by her noble dog whom I remembered.

During my short visit in 1946, Vienna had a totally different ambience from Prague at this time. The four-nation occupying forces made themselves felt all over town by the constant arrival of noisy jeeps, each carrying four soldiers, representing French, American, British, and Russian armies there to keep the peace. In Vienna I stayed with my parents' old friend, Karl Fried. Karl was a *Mischling*—that is, his mother was Aryan and his father Jewish. Since his wife, Steffi, whom we all adored because she was so delightfully intelligent, warm, and funny, had four Jewish grandparents and was therefore unacceptable to Nazi law, they had divorced so that he could keep his Viennese law practice. After her ordeals of sweeping the snow from Vienna's streets under supervision of Nazi guards, and a terrifying escape over the Pyrenees, Steffi emigrated safely to New York. In the middle of the war, Karl married a woman who was Steffi's absolute double. When I arrived in Vienna, Karl's new wife had just given birth, and they were over-joyed with the Czech food I brought them. But while I was glad to see them, I found my visit in this household very troublesome. I remembered Karl and Steffi's close com-panionship and the happy time when the two of them had danced in our drawing room in Troppau during one of my parents' New Year's Eve parties. I worried about Steffi alone in New York.

In the summer of 1946, I accompanied a friend for a lovely week to one of the lakes in the Bohemian forest near Sušice, and sometimes I went with Hedy to visit her parents in Liberec in the Giant Mountains. There we enjoyed the countryside, walking and talking with Hedy's dashing brother, Edmund, who had fought with the Yugoslav parti-sans at the end of the war and who was now studying engineering at Charles University.

In this way, I occupied my time for more than a year, while pleading every week with the British consulate to grant me an entrance visa. I came to know, and to hate, the Czech official in the outer office. His protuberant eyes sheltered by neither brows nor lashes haunted my dreams. Meanwhile, my mother tried to pull every string she could on the other side of the Channel. A thick wad of correspon-dence testifies to her efforts to enable me to return to England during these fourteen months. She had introduc-tions to various prominent British citizens who were sup-posed to be able to help. Among these possible saviors were the conductor Sir Adrian Boult and Lord Samuel, the Liberal leader of the House of Lords, long known for his work with refugees. The answer was always the same: the visa must come from Prague; nothing could be done in England.

One day as I stood weeping at the window of the British Council library, Edwin Muir happened to walk through the room and hesitantly asked what was the matter. On reflection it seems totally out of character for him to have done so, as he would not normally intrude on someone's tears. I confided something of my situation and told him that I had been trying to return to England for more than a year and was unable to obtain a visa. He merely nodded and disappeared, but after a while the chief administrator of the council called me into his office. He made me repeat my story. Then he picked up the telephone and called the British consul. "Bill," he said, "this is Jim. I have a Miss Groag here in the office. She needs a visa so that she can join her mother in London." There was a brief murmur at the other end of the phone. The chief administrator turned to me and said, "Take your passport, go to the consulate, and ask for Mr. C. He is expecting you now."

I put on my coat and went across to the consulate. I told the Czech minion that Mr. C. was expecting me. Wordlessly, I was ushered through a door that had always been firmly closed. Within three minutes, I was outside again, with the priceless stamp in my passport. I sailed past the man in the outer office without a glance. Although it had taken more than a year, I had learned one of the most cynical lessons of life. It's who you know that matters.

With the long-sought-after visa in my passport and nothing preventing my return to England, I was forced to come to terms with the human tie that was most difficult to break.

During the entire fourteen months I had been in this sad and wonderful city, I had seen a great deal of Julian. My feelings for him had not altered since our first encounters in Wales three years earlier. Ignoring the dire warnings about the danger of the Red Army, still much in evidence in Prague at that time, which had a reputation of rape, looting, and other unspeakable habits, I spent many days and nights wandering safely through the town in Julian's company.

We walked for hours through the city's splendid streets and flower-perfumed nights. We talked and talked and talked. We supped in small restaurants and in gardens whose lights were beguilingly reflected in the waters of Prague's fabled river. We rowed on the Vltava in small boats and were enchanted by the spring blossoms that completely covered one of its banks. We went to the theater and to the opera, and we saw many films. We listened to concerts and to lectures on English literature. Through my job, we had privileged access to all British Council entertainments. We were deeply moved by the wonderful performance of Trevor Howard and Celia Johnson in *Brief Encounter*.

I wondered whether Julian sought me out because we were able to speak in English, a language we both found happily suited to our mode of thought, about England and English things. Unlike many of our fellow refugees in the Czech school in Wales, we had both felt at home with English reticence. Now in Prague, we looked avidly for English literary and dramatic events to feed the need we had for something we were afraid of losing. At this time, as the Czech republic was attempting to re-establish its autonomy, everyone else in Prague was imbued with such formidable nationalism and political drive that Julian may have found my lack of both of these tendencies a comforting respite from the world around us. As he was studying political economy, he was in fact receiving a double dose of politics both in the city's atmosphere and in the university lecture rooms.

Our friendship remained exactly as it was during the years at the school at Abernant Lake Hotel. Julian willingly walked miles to escort me back to Hedy's apartment on the outskirts of the city in the suburb of Břevnov. Then he walked back alone, again crossing the city, to his own room in a student hostel. One night as we strolled through the suburban streets heavily scented with the blossom of shimmering white syringa hedges, we met a tipsy Mongolian soldier in Red Army uniform. He courteously asked us the time while waving his arms with at least four watches strapped to each of his wrists. At last, we assured each other, we have a demonstration of the truth of the myth that, while not understanding how to use them, Russian soldiers are entranced by gadgets, and especially by clocks. On another occasion, in the park, a street photographer took our picture and Julian inscribed four copies for me with tantalizing and amusing comments. On one copy he wrote: "A document to show what Miss G. looks like when she pretends not to get the joke." On another he listed, in excruciating detail, the dates of the seven most tense interruptions of our friendship. But while he seemed to be very content with our relationship, I was in a state of constant tumult. Julian gave me unlimited amounts of his time and conversation, yet he never so much as touched my cheek, let alone any other part of my body.

Throughout the year in Prague, I had several short romantic episodes with various other men. A student at the university took me out to dance and dine. His large, handsome, blond presence was intriguing for a few evenings, and his clever moonlighting work in a butcher's shop produced some delicious unrationed meat and sausages for the larder I shared with Hedy. Two of the young men who had been in the school in England also seemed to find me more interesting now that we were independent. They visited me in our apartment, and we spent the odd evenings sipping beer or wine in cheerful cafés overlooking the lights on the river or the busy streets in the town center. A uniformed officer in the Czech security police, encountered at one of the dances we attended, was another of my conquests; he took me dancing in the open air restaurants that abounded near the river. His stiff booted steps, the rough texture of his green uniform, with the gun in its holster on his belt, produced a confusing reaction in me while we swayed about the dance floor. He presented me with a sentimentally inscribed portrait of himself, which I looked at with a sense of shock whenever I came upon it later. What could I have wanted with this man? I wondered.

What I wanted with all of these men was to indulge the sensuality that Julian denied me. In each case, I discovered that while I enjoyed the initial excitement of desiring and being desired, after a very short while it became clear that the face and body being proferred were really quite undesirable. Without the overwhelming combined physical and intellectual need I felt for Julian, the game was not worth the candle. Present or absent, without the least overt sensuality on his part, he stirred my senses so that even the hours spent in his company were like a continuing blurred dream. Nonetheless, we both knew that while I was still as much in love with him as I had been in Wales three years earlier, our relationship could not change. Besides, I needed to make a life for myself. The time had come for me to leave.

It was not until some forty years later, when I was living on the other side of the world and in the midst of writing these memories, that Julian, in one of his letters, offered an explanation for his behavior when we were young. "I enjoyed your company immensely," he wrote, "but was not yet ready for anything really serious, and did not think you deserved anything less than serious—did not cast you as what you call a 'sexual guinea pig.' Take it as a mark of esteem, however misguided. And then, I felt that once our relationship had passed a certain point, there would be no turning back for either of us, and that I couldn't tie you to myself when there was nothing to tie onto, beyond four shirts, a room in a students' hostel, and a very uncertain future." It seems we were both prisoners of our time and upbringing.

At the end of October 1946, then, with the precious British visa in my passport, I was ready to abandon Prague for London. I was longing to return to England, but was leaving my friends and the country to which I had flown with such high hopes. I made a round of farewell visits to all my companions from the school in Wales and to other old friends who had helped me through that difficult year in Prague.

To give me an opportunity to see Paris, my mother had arranged for me to stay there for a week en route to London. She had recently looked after a young Parisian girl called Fleur who was visiting England, and Fleur's mother was willing to return the favor: to house and feed me in her apartment on the place d'Alma. I was aware that Parisians still had great problems getting enough to eat. By the autumn of 1946, although very expensive, food was more plentiful in Czechoslovakia, particularly if one knew where to look for it. A few months earlier, I had taken jars of pork dripping, sausages, butter, and cheese, which had been received like rare and precious jewels, from Prague to Vienna. So I put together various items of useful provender that would not spoil easily to take to my Parisian hostess. I had two large cheeses of at least five kilos, three large salamis, and a bag full of apples.

My two suitcases heavily laden, I arrived with Julian at the Prague Wilson Station (named after the American president) to join a section of the Orient Express on its way from Constantinople to Paris. I was quite overcome at Julian's suggestion that he should see me onto the train and looked forward with ambivalent emotions to being alone with him at this moment.

The Orient Express drew into the platform. We found my reserved seat in its compartment and stowed my luggage on the rack. Then we stood on the platform in that heavy and depressing manner signaling departure. Julian was better at it than most people I have known—his eloquence never flagged—but even he was losing ground. After half an hour, the loudspeaker announced that we were waiting for a connection from Warsaw that would arrive two hours later. We were encouraged to go into the station restaurant to while away the time. We left my luggage comfortably stowed in the compartment and had a wonderful meal of rabbit in a sweet and sour cream sauce and a glass of Pilsner beer, followed by plum dumplings. Throughout we talked as though there were no tomorrow. After an hour, we sauntered back to the train to check on my luggage. The platform was totally deserted, and we stared aghast at two endless gleaming rails. The train had disappeared and my luggage with it.

We never discovered exactly what had happened. We assumed that we simply had not heard the announcement, that the Polish connection had arrived, and that the train had left. There was nothing for it but to book me another seat on the Orient Express for the following day. We asked the stationmaster to phone the Czech-German border station at Cheb, where we assumed my luggage would be taken off the train as the customs men came to make their inspection. He was assured that this would be done. I then telegraphed my hostess in Paris to inform her of the delay and phoned Hedy to tell her that she would have to put up with me for another night. The next morning Julian and I repeated the whole procedure at the Wilson Station. This time I sat stolidly in my compartment in order not to miss the train again. Our farewells were an anticlimax.

No one can repeat such emotion-fraught goodbyes, within twenty-four hours. But as the train was about to pull out, Julian kissed my hand. It was the only time he ever touched me.

When the train arrived in Cheb and the customs officers came on board, I asked to be taken to the customs shed to retrieve my two cases. The man in charge was away having his lunch, and his assistant was adamant that my luggage was not there, claiming that it must have been sent on to Paris. We argued for a while, as I told him that I had been assured it would be stored in his shed to await my arrival, but he insisted he could not find it, and in the end I had to go back onto the train, as I feared it would again leave without me. I did not believe that the cases would have gone straight on to Paris, even if their labels had a Paris address, so when a few yards further on the train stopped again, this time at the German border, I descended once more and insisted that the customs men should search their shed for my luggage. Again, nothing was found, and I decided that I would have to repeat this maneuver at the German-French border.

My activity and consternation had intrigued the other passengers in my compartment, and we soon discussed the mystery of my missing luggage and how it came to be lost. Everyone became involved in my predicament and had good advice. To lose two suitcases in central Europe in the autumn of 1946 was hardly a minor disaster. Even if one had large amounts of money, which I did not, one could not simply go into a shop and buy what one wanted. All material goods were extremely scarce. My missing suitcases contained not only precious food for my French hostess, and some presents for my mother and several English friends, but all my clothes, which at this time of textile shortages and rationing were extremely valuable. My friend Hanni's mother, Tante Boeszi, had sewn me two or three dresses and some priceless blouses made of contraband parachute silk. It had been easier for me to discover black-market items in Prague than it would be in my respectable English milieu, where I had no connections of this sort.

At Strasbourg, I again repeated my discussion with customs men, on both the German and the French side of the border. Nowhere were my cases to be found.

A young Jewish soldier from Palestine was particularly interested in my story, and we began to chat about our wartime experiences. As the day turned into night, my excursions to German and French customs sheds became ever more depressing and it seemed clear that my luggage was unlikely to be found. At the same time the soldier's interest in me deepened and his attentions became more pressing. I was unnerved by what was to be my final separation from Julian, and by the loss of my belongings, and felt that I didn't care too much what happened next. The soldier's exploring hands under cover of the darkness in the crowded compartment were almost a consoling diversion.

Finally we drew into the Gare de l'Est in Paris. With very little hope, I went to the station authorities and asked about unaccompanied luggage from Czechoslovakia the previous day. Nothing of the sort had arrived. It was suggested that the luggage might have been taken to the Gare du Nord, the Paris station where all lost luggage for the whole city was stored. The soldier, Geza, had stayed with me during my questioning of the station personnel. He could see that I was far too tired to go anywhere else and suggested that he should escort me at once to Madame de Fougères at the place d'Alma.

My first appearance at Madame's apartment was hardly designed to inspire confidence. I was travel-stained and weary, had no luggage whatsoever, and was accompanied by a rather scruffy, unshaved soldier, who was not even an officer. Madame lived with her aristocratic sister. Dressed in unrelieved black, they were two impoverished middle-aged ladies, whose situation was exacerbated by the exigencies of the war. Their genteel poverty was in stark contrast to their residence. The place d'Alma is, after all, one of the most elegant Parisian corners, overlooking the Seine at the pont d'Alma. My new companion from Palestine took his leave as quickly as he could and promised to help me the next day in tracking down my bags at the Gare du Nord.

Meanwhile, I tried to explain to the ladies in my best French how I came to be a day late and in such disarray. Although I had heard horror stories of catastrophic French situations during the Nazi occupation of Paris, these women lived an extremely sheltered existence. Compared to my English teachers and friends, Madame and her sister were like characters out of a Balzac novel. They seemed incapable of imagining my independent travel from London to Prague and my autonomous life there for the past year. They showed me photographs of their lovely Fleur in a flower-studded meadow and described her lyrically as a "poem of a girl." They offered to lend me some of her clothes while I was waiting for mine, and we found a blouse, coat, and skirt that fitted reasonably well. I was touched that they were willing to entrust me with the "poem's" garments, as I felt that they viewed me as a rather unsavory character.

But more uncomfortable than my lack of clothes or toothbrush was the fact that I was eating and depriving them of their unbelievably stark rations. Their genteel background and their location in a capital city meant that they had connections neither with the black market nor with the peasants who managed to supply a large part of the population in most parts of the war-devastated world. Moreover, the German occupation had seen to it that France did not have the well-organized rationing system that had kept Britain adequately fed since 1939. For most of the meals I had with them, the ladies produced plain potatoes, sometimes with an onion or a carrot. There was neither meat, cheese, nor butter. We drank coffee made of acorns. I thought longingly and despairingly of the cheese and salami I had bought to repay their hospitality, tossed about somewhere in my old suitcases.

The next day my Palestine soldier friend phoned, and we arranged to go to the other station to search for my luggage. No one had seen or heard of it. At this point I sent a telegram to Julian in Prague telling him what had happened and asking him to try the Czech customs at Cheb once again. Then I settled down to making the most of my Paris sojourn.

Madame found a friend of Fleur's called Denise, who took me sightseeing to the famous landmarks of the city, which, though beautiful, I found less moving and architecturally exciting than Prague. On Sunday Geza offered to accompany me to Versailles. It happened to be the first of November, commemorated throughout the Catholic world as All Saints Day. The suburban train to Versailles was filled with people dressed in black, carrying large bouquets of white chrysanthemums, descending at every station to visit local cemeteries. Louis XIV's palace at Versailles was overwhelmingly large and run-down, and the gray somberness of this November day corresponded well with the funereal atmosphere of remembered souls. I was glad to return to Paris and to accept the soldier's offer of a meal. I was less glad when it became clear that he also expected me to go to bed with him afterwards. I left him sitting there, in front of the half-eaten dinner, so much more substantial than the ladies' fare at the place d'Alma, to which I returned hungry and dispirited.

After two more days of uncomfortable waiting for news from Prague, I finally received a telegram from Julian. He wrote: "Luggage safe, forwarded from Cheb, Friday or

Saturday express, meet train or enquire station." So it had been at the Czech border, as the man in Prague had promised, after all. I could hardly wait to present my hostesses with the food I had brought for them, and I imagined their expressions as they beheld the cheese and salami. The next day I went with Fleur's friend Denise to collect it. The sight of my two old suitcases was heartwarming. The French station officials made me open them at once to ensure that everything was in order. Right on top of the first case was a note in Czech. It informed me that in order to avoid spoilage, all edible items had been removed from the luggage. Another mystery of the Orient Express was solved. The customs officers in Cheb were having a feast.

PART IV

ENGLAND AGAIN: OR LEARNING TO WALK

CHAPTER
7

As I sat in the boat train traveling from Dover to London's Victoria Station, the exquisite greenness of the fields and hedgerows rolling by the window caught at my throat as they would over and over again whenever I arrived in England from California in future years. I felt a great sense of relief and peace at the thought of being again in the place that had offered me such generous hospitality. But at Victoria, the passion of my mother's embrace symbolized years of her pent-up emotion and anxiety. It was in fact the first time since we had left Czechoslovakia as emigrés in 1939 that I sensed a greater closeness between us. Moreover, I felt that there was more than relief about my safe return after a year of uncertainty. She was excited about something else.

Just before the end of the war, Chris and Iris's house, Waxham, had been badly damaged by a bomb. My mother, with the rest of the household, had been sleeping in the cellar. There, she and Afra, one of the family friends, had appropriated a small part of the coal cellar for their sleeping quarters. No one was physically harmed by this bomb, but the experience left them all considerably shaken. Since the house was unfit for human habitation, Chris and Iris had rented a smaller one nearby, but now they no longer had enough space for the extended boarding family that had made their household such a boon to so many people. For almost two years, my mother had been living in a room in Croydon and had become accustomed to living by herself.

As I looked about the familiar concourse at Victoria Station, I assumed we would be taking a train straight down to Croydon to stay in her room or that I might be put up by Chris and Iris for a little while. Instead, my mother mysteriously beckoned a taxi outside the station and gave the driver some unknown address. When I questioned our destination, she said that it was a secret. We drove a short distance towards Chelsea, and the cab delivered us to the front door of a medium-sized block of redbrick flats in a small street between the King's Road and a tall gray Victorian Gothic church surrounded by a sizable churchyard with splendid large trees. The taxi dismissed, we entered the building whose name, MERIDEN COURT, was displayed in large white letters above the front door. I was surprised to hear the porter, sitting in his cubbyhole by the front door, greet my mother by name. She then surprised me even more by taking a key out of her handbag and opening the door of the flat nearest the lift. She ushered me into the small hallway of the flat and then into a large empty room, saying, "Welcome home."

I was stunned by the significance of what I saw. "Do you really mean this is ours?" My mother could barely nod with suppressed excitement. I began to poke about the small flat, which felt like a palace. The large, almost square room with a bedroom-sized alcove was bathed in the late afternoon sunlight; outside the window was a small refreshing strip of garden, and there was a well-appointed kitchen and bathroom. Hot water came from a main boiler in the building and gushed noisily out of the taps when I tried them. There were several large built-in cupboards in the hall and kitchen. But the most satisfying and delicious asset was the front door to which only we had the key. Gradually, I assimilated the fact that, after years of living in other people's houses, we finally had a place of our own.

For a short while longer, we admired the charm of our new home, including the only two items of furniture that stood in it: a narrow eighteenth-century walnut desk and a small rounded armchair. Then, regretfully, we decided we had better return to my mother's room in Croydon, where we would have to sleep for the next two weeks until we had found enough furniture to settle into the flat.

In the train on our way down to Croydon, my mother told me how it had happened that this wonderful little treasure was to be ours. Just before my return to England, one of those happy circumstances from which we had benefited throughout our emigré experience had come her way. Miss Bolton, a client of the firm of solicitors for which my mother had been working during the past four years, had rented the flat in Meriden Court as a pied-à-terre. Recently, she had bought a small house further down the King's Road in Bywater Street and now suggested that she would transfer her flat to my mother. Moreover, to make it possible for my mother to afford it on her meager salary, Miss Bolton would continue the rent at the same wartime level, which was far lower than the rents commanded by central London real estate at this time of horrendous housing shortages, and simply sublet to us. The desk and chair left in the flat were on loan to us as Miss Bolton did not have room for them in her Bywater Street house.

This was a magnificent homecoming indeed. My mother was clearly elated to have me back in England and to be able to make a future based on a hopeful stability after seven years of exiled uncertainty.

The next few weeks flew by in a dizzying whirl of planning and new experiences. Not only were we getting ready to move into the flat and finding basic furniture wherever we could, but also my own future had to be considered. As I had opted for an idealistic plunge to rebuild Czechoslovakia instead of continuing with my English pre-university studies, we now felt that a university education, even if I could get some sort of scholarship, would strain my mother's resources too long and that I had better find a speedier way of earning a living.

Through her affiliation with the Business and Professional Women's Club, my mother had met people involved in the London School of Stenotyping and had suggested to me while I was still in Prague that this might be something suitable for me. Despite the problems I had encountered in Prague, I had enjoyed my independence there and was eager to become self-supporting. So it was arranged that I should attend the London School of Stenotyping as soon as the next term started. And I began my daily journey to the school's headquarters at the corner of High Holborn and the Aldwych. Stenotyping is the shorthand machine method of verbatim reporting during law court proceedings, and, because it is phonetic, it can be used in any language for simultaneous translation. I was quite intrigued by this idea and looked forward to using my four languages. Within a few weeks, I had proved myself to be a fairly proficient student. The principal of the school told me that by the end of the course I would have a choice of jobs: either to teach at the school or to take a rather special position with an international organization in Geneva. Life seemed to be settling down very simply and easily.

Soon I began to visit my old friends in various parts of Sussex and Surrey, and I often went to see my St. Clair school friend Sheila, who was working on her mathematics degree at London University and lived in a boardinghouse in Swiss Cottage. In this house lived also a number of other students, who took me into their circle, particularly one of the young men, a Viennese refugee, Gerry, who was an engineering student at Queen Mary College. Gerry had come to England alone at age sixteen, had been interned on the Isle of Man as an "enemy alien" like all Austrian and German Jewish refugees, and later served in the Pioneer Corps of the British army. He was a sensitive young man, with a very dry and quirky sense of humor, and a gifted amateur violinist. Gerry had some idea that my year alone abroad had turned me into a sophisticated and sexually experienced cosmopolitan. He could hardly have been more wrong. In any case, we began to see a fair amount of each other, and he often came to our flat in Chelsea, where he was spectacularly helpful with the mechanics of getting organized in a new place.

One of our pleasures was the exploration of our new neighborhood. Chelsea, and particularly the King's Road, was a world apart. Although everything from the exterior of the buildings to the surfaces of the roads was in great need of repair, the charm of this part of London cast its unique spell, especially after living in various country or suburban areas of England. In its way, Chelsea was at that time still something of a village, with the King's Road its main shopping street, densely filled with family butchers, greengrocers, bakers, and ironmongers, apart from the usual English small-town chain stores like Boots, Timothy White's, Woolworth, and Marks and Spencer. These stores, interspersed with innumerable antique shops and small restaurants, led up to the genteel refinement of Peter Jones at Sloane Square.

The side streets leading from the King's Road, whether down to the river or away from it, were a feast for the eye even in their state of postwar dilapidation. There were little nineteenth-century terraced houses and some quite large detached redbrick houses from the nineteen thirties with tidy front gardens and garages; then again, there were elegant buildings from the turn of the century like those in the Vale and Mulberry Walk and interesting pieces of earlier nineteenth-century domestic architecture in Glebe Place. Finally, there were the fine houses of famous artists, like Turner's overlooking the Thames reach and Rossetti's along the embankment in Cheyne Walk; there was Carlyle's house in Cheyne Row, and the sad emptiness of Tite Street, once the home of Oscar Wilde, Whistler, and Augustus John. Here we could still see Edward Godwin's wonderful White House, designed for Whistler, and briefly rented by the famous Lady Warwick. Only gradually did we discover who the innumerable famous literary and artistic inhabitants of Chelsea had been, but the intriguing variety of its architecture made an immediate and deep impression. In close proximity to our own new home in Chelsea Manor Street, we had the parallel charm of Astell Street, named after the seventeenth-century feminist Mary Astell, who had once lived in Chelsea's Paradise Walk, and next to this comfortable middle-class road lay the tiny terraced cottages of Godfrey Street, once the homes of working men and women, now as much sought after as the mews behind grand and elegant London houses. On the other side of the churchyard were the turn-of-the-century council flats, dark and uncomfortable-looking, which, as we learned much later, were not to receive individual bathrooms until the nineteen seventies. Until then their inhabitants were forced to bathe in a tub that was mostly covered with a large heavy wooden slab that served as their kitchen table.

My mother and I spent many fine weekends exploring these Chelsea streets, and during the forty years she lived in Meriden Court, we never tired of wandering about the neighborhood. During this period, while living with my mother, I discovered that she loved her work and her independent life in London. She seemed to get a good deal of satisfaction out of doing her job as a tax and trust accountant for her firm. It was obvious from the occasions when she took me to her office that she was greatly appreciated by the partners of the firm as well as by her colleagues, the clerks, and the rest of the office staff. When some years later, Mary, a new young solicitor, was taken on by the firm, she and my mother worked together and became friends, and the younger woman told me often that my mother had taught her all the finer details of her job.

London also, with all its cultural amenities, was a most satisfying milieu for my mother. I had always suspected that she would have preferred to live in Vienna, rather than in the provinces. Now she was in her element. It was as though she had hungered for the kind of cultural feasts she found close at hand. She spent much time in art galleries, at concerts, and in the theater whenever she could afford to do so. And she and her old friends also enjoyed many weekend hours wandering through the extensive London parks, sometimes blazing with color, but always tranquil. Six of her women friends from Troppau had managed to escape and settle in London, and these women, some with, some without husbands, had a wonderful time exploring their new surroundings and creating new lives. She also made many new friends, in the neighborhood, through her work, and through the women's clubs she joined. She often told me of the pleasure it gave her to know that the life she had now forged for herself was built on her own earnings and achieved by her own labor. The flower man whose colorful stall she passed at the corner of the King's Road every time she returned home knew her well, and she once told me that if she still had all the money she had spent on his flowers she would be rich. I don't think she missed her five servants for a moment, but she did employ a cleaning woman to come in once a week as soon as she could afford

one. During these years in London, several men had proposed marriage, but, as she said to me occasionally, "Why
should I take on an old man whom I will have to nurse,
when my life is so good and pleasant and I can support
myself?"

During the first few months after my return to
England, I settled down to my studies at the stenotyping
school and widened my friendships with old and new companions. I went out with various young men whom I met
through my old schoolfriends and occasionally the sons of
my mother's friends and acquaintances. Gerry became a
steady companion. His interest in music and his activities
as an amateur violinist brought me close to his chamber
music colleagues, and we spent many evenings at the Albert
and Wigmore halls listening to concerts and walking around
the London parks.

It was as I rose to my feet after a resounding performance of Beethoven's Emperor concerto in the Albert Hall
that I first experienced a paralyzing pain in my right instep.
We had to sit down again for a few minutes while the
audience filed out of the building until I was able to walk
home. I forgot about this pain fairly quickly and went about
my business not giving it a thought. A few weeks later
Gerry and I visited Chris and Iris, who had moved to their
new home in Juniper Hall in Surrey, where Chris was now
directing the local work of the Society for the Promotion
of Field Studies. We all walked through the wonderful countryside around Juniper Hall, Mickleham, and Box Hill,
climbing over styles and along hedgerows. At one point we
had to jump over a narrow stream. As I came down, with
all my weight onto my right foot after the leap, I again
experienced the excruciating pain I had felt at the Albert
Hall concert. It subsided after a few moments, and we
enjoyed the remainder of our visit while Chris regaled us
with stories of the history of Juniper Hall, which had been

the place of refuge for aristocrats who had fled the French Revolution in the late eighteenth century. Madame de Staël among others had stayed in this delightful country house, and Fanny Burney and her aristocratic French husband, Monsieur d'Arblay, had lived in a small cottage a few steps away in the village of Mickleham.

Within the next weeks, I began to feel ill and nauseous with an uncomfortably high temperature every night. The doctor who visited me guessed at all kinds of stomach infections, including typhoid, and, after three weeks without change in my condition, packed me off to St. George's Hospital at Hyde Park Corner. Thus began a new and very different chapter in my life.

St. George's was one of the best teaching hospitals in London, with every possible consulting specialist at hand. I was confined to bed, where I remained without ever placing a foot on the floor for the next three months. As the specialists ruled out one disease after another and my temperature continued to swing from normal to about 103 degrees every evening, the general consensus was that I was suffering from tuberculosis, though no TB was found in all their examinations. Every so often I was asked whether I had any other symptoms apart from the nausea. When I mentioned the occasional pain I had had in my foot, I was firmly told that first we must deal with the nausea and temperature and that I wasn't to worry my pretty little head about the pain in my foot.

As I was in central London, it was easy for my mother and Gerry and all my friends to visit. They came faithfully with books and flowers, and I also became quite friendly with several of the young nurses and medical students who got to know me well over these three months. Towards the end of the third month, my temperature finally subsided (apparently because of my immobilization), and after I had

spent a week totally free from fever, the doctors announced
that I might get out of bed.

Supported by two nurses, I climbed out of bed and
was urged to walk across the ward. As I put my weight on
my right foot, I let out an involuntary cry of pain, but the
nurses, thinking I was exaggerating my weakness after three
months in bed, insisted that I walk across the room. After
the ten necessary steps to accomplish this, my right foot
had swollen to double its size. Everyone was impressed,
and the doctor called to the scene ordered an immediate X-
ray of my foot. When the orthopedic specialist examined
the films, a diagnosis was finally established. I was suffering
from a TB lesion of the tarsal joint. This accounted for the
pain, the nausea, and the temperature. The treatment was
to be one to two years of immobilization of the joint in a
plaster cast, the first year to be spent entirely in bed. The
doctors assured my mother and me that with this treatment
a complete recovery of the foot was almost certain.

After three months at St. George's, I was sent to its
annex, the Atkinson Morley Hospital in Wimbledon. There,
when Princess Elizabeth was married in Westminster
Abbey, we listened to the wedding on the wireless. As a
Christmas treat, Gerry brought his friend Steve and Steve's
fiancée, Hilary, who gave us a spirited performance of some
Schubert trios. As an encore Steve produced a vibrant ren-
dering of "the Swan" for the fierce old lady in the bed next
to mine; as with the wedding of the princess, there was not
a dry eye in the place. Patients from several other wards
came to join us, as did the doctors and nurses, who lounged
informally on our beds while they listened to the
performance.

Quite soon after Christmas, I was transferred to Heatherwood Hospital in Ascot dealing only with orthopedic
cases. I didn't know what to expect from an orthopedic
hospital. On arriving in the ambulance, with my foot in its

plaster cast up the knee, I was wheeled into a seemingly endless ward of what turned out to be thirty beds, with one of its long walls consisting of glass doors that were almost always open to the elements. I was surprised to see that I was the only patient in this ward who was to lie in a real bed. All the other women were stretched out on narrow constructions that looked like ironing boards on wheels. I discovered later that these were in fact plaster casts molded to their backs and supported by wooden frames. Every one of the other patients was suffering from tuberculosis of the spine or the hip. I was marvelously fortunate to have this lesion in the tarsal joint in the middle of my foot. This meant that in contrast to all the others, who had to lie spread-eagled on their backs for two to three years, I was able to lie on my side and curl up in bed, almost as I did before my foot was entombed in its cast.

I looked around me with interest at these people who were to become my companions for what then seemed to be an interminably long time. They were of all ages and appeared to be fairly content with their lot. They chatted and knitted and read and soon told me that every so often we would have a get together with the men's ward for a whist drive, which I could not quite imagine for those stretched out on the plaster-molded trolleys. In fact, these trolleys moved on comfortable wheels, and their occupants were extremely adept at making their toilette, combing their hair, knitting, and even playing cards, just as they had promised. For these card games in the men's ward, all kinds of titivating took place, and the trolleys were arranged with the patients' heads together in a starlike constellation, their feet stretched out in the opposite directions. The games worked well, and many romances blossomed on those afternoons.

The truth about TB in the joints, or "bovine" TB as it was called then, is that it was a slow and boring disease.

Once encased in our plaster casts, there was no pain. The cure was simply complete immobilization of the diseased joint for a very long time, good food, and lots of fresh air. After I had been in this Ascot hospital for a few months, the doctor who had us in his regular care went off on a vacation. His stand-in was a young Scot who came straight from his hospital training in Aberdeen. I was becoming somewhat tired of the lengthy cure and grumbled to the new doctor about these wasted years out of my life. He bent over the bed, looked me straight in the eye, and delivered a comforting medical opinion. "You are lucky, lassie," he told me, "that you are in England. In Scotland we don't believe in this rest cure. If you were up there in my part of the world, we wouldn't waste your time like this. We would have cut off your foot long ago." It was a long time before I grumbled about my treatment again.

Nevertheless, my mother and Gerry were still busy on my behalf. Gerry's father, who lived in New York at this time, wrote to say that in the United States TB of the bone was now being treated with streptomycin, which cured the disease within a matter of weeks, and that he would send this drug over to England for me. My mother had long discussions with my doctors in the Ascot hospital and with Mr. Burns, the Harley Street specialist who had first diagnosed the problem at St. George's. Every English doctor had the same answer. "We are almost a hundred percent certain that we can cure your daughter's foot with our treatment, even though it will take two years. Streptomycin is a new drug. It has not been tried long enough for us to know what side effects it may have. Even though it appears to cure TB in a matter of weeks or at least months, we will not risk it." I was forced to resign myself to the two years of incarceration.

Reflecting on this period of my life, I now realize that its tedious, seemingly interminable, forced idleness gave me

ot have learned, that stood me
is patience. The knowledge that
eventually come to an end makes
earable. In later periods, when others
bited intolerance and furious impatience, I
myself imperturbable and thought how such
e wasted precious energy.

Although I was reasonably content to be in the large
ward with the companions surrounding me, there was one
maddening aspect of this life that I found hard to accept. At
this time, very soon after the war, hospitals were primitively
equipped. We received tolerably edible food and as much
fresh air as was deemed healthy for us. We were gently and
comfortingly nursed by a team of cheerful and friendly
nurses. But we also received a dose of entertainment that I
hated. The ward was fitted out with one solitary radio with
loudspeakers at various points. It was always set at the
BBC's program of light entertainment. After a while, this
type of music blaring away throughout the day became
more than I could bear. The sister in charge took pity on
me and came to suggest an alternative.

There was a small side room with only three beds in
it, she told me. "This room is usually reserved for patients
who are very seriously ill. At the moment we luckily don't
have any such cases. The room is occupied by two middle-
aged ladies who also can't stand the music in the main
ward. If you like you may join them. But you will exchange
noise for age. And I must warn you that these two ladies
are quite testy and prickly." I was delighted at this offer
and decided to risk the testiness of middle age. Forthwith
my bed was wheeled into the small side ward.

I had moved not only to another age bracket, but also
to another class. My two new companions spoke in refined
middle-class accents, and they read bound books in contrast
to the magazines, called books by the people in the large

ward. Deferring to our enforced intimacy, they allo
to call them by their first names, something they c
would not have done had we met under more usual c
stances. So they were Elcy and Dorothy and I was Su
I was sure that they had discussed this problem of nan
before I was wheeled in to them. Obviously, Sister ha
asked whether they would mind having such a young thing
as myself in their room and had assured them that I was
housetrained and would not behave like an adolescent
hooligan.

Both Elcy and Dorothy were spread-eagled flat on their
backs on their ironing boards. They read continuously and
discussed their novels and biographies with each other. Elcy
lay in the middle of us three, Dorothy was on her left, and
I on her right. Elcy wore a dull silver bracelet that gleamed
strangely on the suntanned arm that protruded from her
white hospital gown. Both she and Dorothy had inquisitive
dark brown eyes, and these four searching eyes were
intensely interested in me and my visitors. They asked endless questions about my childhood and my friends; they
talked to my mother when she came to visit me; and they
were ostentatiously discreet when Gerry arrived, as he did
twice a week with his bouquet of roses and an endless supply of entertaining books.

Early on in my illness, I had thought that Gerry was
becoming too attached to me and I was not at all sure that
this was a good idea for our future. I told him very firmly
that I did not want him to come to see me in St. George's
Hospital. However, I gathered years later from my dear
Tante Grete, whom we saw often in London, that despite
my own feelings, my mother, still determined to protect my
well-being, had taken it upon herself to ensure Gerry's regular visits, even after I had told him not to come. To visit me
now in the orthopedic hospital in Ascot involved a tiresome
journey on the Green Line bus that took at least an hour

and a half from various parts of London. For my mother this meant a day out of her weekend after a hard week's work; for Gerry two afternoons out of his graduate studies at Queen Mary College. They carefully spaced themselves so that they would not come on the same days, thus giving me as many visiting hours as possible between them. Gerry was eager for me to take some correspondence courses towards a university degree; he brought various materials of sample courses, but I found it impossible to concentrate and to write the necessary essays.

Instead, I spent my time devising my own course on English and European literature and haphazardly read works ranging from Hardy and Meredith to E. M. Delafield, Nancy Mitford, Dorothy Sayers, and Thomas Mann. My writing activities were confined to my correspondence with many friends. Two of my close women friends married while I was in the hospital. My Czech friend Hedy, in the midst of her achitecture studies, married an English architect and came to live in London, and my old school friend Sheila, who had been at St. Clair with me, married a mathematician whom she met while they both worked for the civil service.

I had also been corresponding with Julian, who after my return from Czechoslovakia and throughout the first year of this tedious illness had sent me frequent, interesting, and comforting letters. However, in the early part of March 1948, as I lay there in my hospital bed, came the news that Jan Masaryk, the foreign minister of Czechoslovakia, had been pushed or jumped out of his Prague office window after the communists gained power. Masaryk, the son of the founder president, had been one of the main links with the first Czech republic. He had been in England during the war and was the only member of that government left in the new Czech state. Fearing to cause Julian difficulties with mail arriving from the West, I reluctantly stopped our correspondence. For the next forty years, Julian and I were out of touch, though I always knew more or less where he was, as some of our old schoolfellows kept a roster of our addresses. Then, in 1987, just as I began to write these memories, I heard that Julian, who had remained in Czechoslovakia, was very ill and I wrote him a letter. He replied immediately, describing his own life during the intervening silent years, which seemed to me like a story whose characters resembled those in the plays and novels of Vaclav Havel and Milan Kundera. We again began to correspond, discussing our friendship among other topics.

Not only did my hospital companions, Elcy and Dorothy, benefit from the drama of my visitors, and to some extent from that of my correspondence, but I also became somewhat involved in their lives. Elcy's husband, Jock, was a large placid man who came and sat more or less silently by her bedside. Dorothy was not married, but a brother and ancient mother used to appear at infrequent intervals. On the whole, I thought both Dorothy and Elcy were relieved rather than disappointed when their visitors left.

We had succumbed to that remarkable atmosphere that affects people who are drawn together by a common problem and a forced way of life. We had our jokes, incomprehensible to those "outside." We waited impatiently for Matron's midmorning rounds and her attentive interest in our individual condition. Her visits were almost like a pastoral benediction or the approval of a headmistress. We speculated about the tense friendship and the quarrels of the ward sister and her staff-nurse, both tall, angular women who could make our lives pleasant or hellish depending on their moods. They had a system of marching through the ward together making beds, inspecting patients, and dispensing pills and potions with a military precision that resembled a ballet in modern dress. Every three months one or the other of them would wheel me to the surgery to have my plaster cast changed and my foot X-rayed. That was the extent of my medical activities.

As the months progressed, I realized that one of Elcy's visitors was a delight both to Elcy and to me. This was an elderly lady in her seventies, who came roughly every six weeks and after the first visit settled herself down between Elcy's bed and mine, chatting companionably with both of us. She had faded but intensely penetrating blue eyes and the pale pink complexion that usually accompanies auburn red hair. By now, however, her long hair was snow white and dressed in the fashion of Edwardian days forming a crown around her head with a large bun fastened with silver hairpins at the back. She always wore long flowing dresses and skirts of a soft William Morris blue that enhanced the color of her eyes. She lived in Hertfordshire deep in the country, and her house adjoined the farmland belonging to Elcy's family, so that she had known Elcy as a young girl and was doing her neighborly duty in the most superb and traditional Victorian manner. Not that I understood this at the time. I was simply enchanted with the gaiety of her conversation and the genuine interest she took in all our boring hospital doings and routine. I was quite unaware that she also discovered a great deal about me and my affairs during these visits. When her visiting time was nearly at an end, she used to consult a silver pocket watch to ensure that she would not be late for the cumbersome return journey, first to London and then out to Hertfordshire. She refused to set foot on a bus; having grown up in the days of the railway, she never traveled anywhere except by train. She introduced herself as Mrs. Hammond. She was Lucy Barbara Hammond, and I began to look forward to her visits with great impatience.

In the late spring of 1948, the doctors decided that I

was ready to leave my bed and to begin the second year of the long process of my cure. This meant four stages, each of three months. The first, on crutches in the plaster cast; the second, if the bone was healing well enough, with full weight on the foot, still in its cast; the third, three months again on crutches but now without the cast, and finally, walking on the healed foot. A second year of cure, but at least not in bed, nor in a hospital.

I was jubilant. The long months in hospital beds had become tedious. The hospital's inward-looking world held few charms. With my few belongings packed, my mother took me home in the ambulance to our beloved little flat in Meriden Court. Luckily, it was on the ground floor overlooking the sunny back strip of plantings so that I would not have to worry about stairs. The flat looked and was tiny after the spaciousness of the hospital wards. Even the small ward in Heatherwood Hospital in which I had recently lived with my two middle-aged companions seemed like a ballroom in comparison.

My mother was clearly uncomfortable at the thought of my being cooped up in the small studio flat with my crutches, huge unmanageable sticks, cluttering up the place. It was difficult to hop through the narrow hallway to and from the bathroom, and I too felt dubious about living for the next nine months in this crammed city environment. I had become used to the space and constant fresh air that blew relentlessly into our hospital rooms; and I missed it.

Somehow behind the scenes my mother must have been busy, for one day, soon after my return home, both my old headmistress, Miss Stevens, and our old friends Chris and Iris telephoned. All suggested that I might come and visit them in their country retreats. It was decided that I should stay for about six weeks in each place.

Juniper Hall, a grand old house near Box Hill, was very lively—the ghosts of those French emigrés from the

1789 revolution who had lived there for many years did
not haunt us. It was while I was sitting on a blanket in the
middle of its large circular lawn that Iris brought me a small
white envelope from Barbara Hammond boldly addressed,
as was all her writing, in green ink. It was a sad but wonderfully welcoming letter.

She wrote to tell me that her husband, Lawrence, had
died a short while previously and she wondered whether
I would be willing to keep her company during the rest
of my convalescence to relieve her solitude. She stressed
that Lawrence would have been especially pleased that
they might be of some use to me as he had been "so
miserable about the mean and treacherous way in which
we treated Czechoslovakia in '38," which had cost me my
home.

I did not take very long to make up my mind. After a
consultation with my mother, to whom she had also written
about this plan, I agreed to move to Hertfordshire to live
with Barbara Hammond for a while. We would find out
whether we were as compatible as we had seemed to be
when she sat by my bed and chatted with me during her
visits to Elcy Riddick in the hospital.

I discovered only very gradually what an interesting
household I had entered and who Barbara and Lawrence
Hammond were. I knew nothing of their work or reputa-
tion as historians when I arrived, but as I lived there I
quickly became aware that I had come into an extraordinary
place.

The Hammonds' house, Oatfield, was an enlarged farm
cottage on a quiet country lane at Piccott's End at the edge
of Hemel Hempstead. It was surrounded by a large upward
sloping garden and an even larger field; the upper windows
looked out upon the gently undulating Hertfordshire countryside of fields and trees as far as the eye could see. Very soon
I discovered that worries about the loss of this view through

the possible building of a government-sponsored "New Town" haunted Barbara's waking and sleeping hours.

When I arrived at Oatfield, I was introduced to the household, which at that time consisted of the dog, Rags, a large, energetic gray mongrelly sheepdog who had looked like a bundle of rags when Barbara found him as a lost puppy; an old cat who slept on a specially prepared hot water bottle in the downstairs bathroom and who was forced to wear a bell around his neck in order to warn the birds of his approach; and an elderly couple who lived in the small cottage next door and took care of the house, the garden, and the cooking.

As I was still not able to maneuver myself upstairs on my crutches, it was decided that I should sleep on the sofa in the drawing room, which was also Barbara's study. This lovely room was furnished in hues of faded Morris blue that matched Barbara's inevitable long-skirted blue dress, its walls filled with books and its French windows open to the garden almost constantly, ushering in sweet scents of her roses, wisteria, stocks, and nicotiana.

The garden was Barbara's delight. Nearest the house was a rectangular lawn, closed at one end by a large and very old weeping ash under which we often had afternoon tea. Behind the lawn going up the hill were two splendid beds of old-fashioned roses, backed by a wall of blue and purple delphiniums. Barbara scorned hybrid roses, and the small, softly colored old-fashioned kind were indeed far more suited to her own coloring and to that of the furnishings of her house. Opposite the weeping ash at the other side of the lawn was a side border of small pinks and delicate plants to which Barbara attended herself. Her favorites were the deep blue gentians, which she weeded and nurtured on her knees. Behind the rosebeds, still going uphill, was a large wild garden planted with a mixture of loose-growing plants where columbines and peonies had taken over. A narrow path led up in the center between the rose-beds and the wild garden to the top of the hill where a small seat had been installed. This had been Barbara and Lawrence's favorite place from which to look down upon the garden and the house. It also offered a view over the fields and the surrounding countryside. I too became very fond of this seat, and when the weather was warm enough, I often took my book to read there.

Barbara told me that as a young woman she had suffered from tuberculosis of the kidney and her doctors had recommended fresh air treatment. I assumed that this was another reason why she had become interested in me. As a result of her own illness, she and her husband had bought this house with the intention of living out of doors as much as possible. They had built a small revolving wooden shelter with one side open to the elements, which was still in its place on their spacious lawn, and for most of their married life they had both slept in this shelter except on the iciest nights. She thought I might like to use it also, but I shuddered at the thought. Even Heatherwood's fresh air policy had not been as drastic, and I much preferred the narrow Victorian sofa in the drawing room/study.

So it was that every evening Mrs. Gubb came over from the cottage to prepare our late night drink of Ovaltine and then made up my bed on the sofa in the drawing room. There I slept, very comfortably, surrounded by innumerable tall greenbacked volumes of the *Annual Register* that went back to their beginnings in the eighteenth century.

As I lived there with books squeezed into every available space on walls, in corridors, even piled up on tables and stairs and more arriving by every post from publishers or in large bundles from the London Library, I became aware of the Hammonds' life as scholars. I had never known any scholars to the extent of being part of their household, and I found the ambience strangely fascinating, wishing also that I could absorb something of the inside of all those books and not merely the atmosphere of the house. That is not to say that I did not open any of the books on the Hammonds' shelves. I read as voraciously as I had always done. I still have a little notebook in which I wrote down at least a hundred titles read at Oatfield. Apparently, I read my way systematically through all the nineteenth-century novels the Hammonds had used to research their own works, and any others I could find scattered throughout the house. Occasionally I also shared Barbara's new books from the London Library, as well as the new offerings written by her friends. Thus I learned something of the interesting feminist authors who later came to mean much more to me. I read Mary Stocks's book on Eleanor Rathbone and Mary Agnes Hamilton's novels. I struggled with Orwell's *1984*, recently published, and remember astounding Barbara's visitors by saying that I could empathize with Kafka's feeling of bewilderment since I had experienced something of the problems of confronting an unconfrontable bureaucracy in Prague. But the scholarly books that the Hammonds and their friends had created—what I thought of as the "serious" books—seemed out of my range.

Barbara's solicitous friends came to visit her frequently. Every weekend someone arrived to comfort her in her solitude now that Lawrence had died. They were all deeply concerned, first because the marriage had been so close, and second because they wanted to encourage Barbara to continue with the research on the book about London's open spaces and public parks, which she had been working on for some years. I was amazed at their matter-of-fact inclusion of a complete ignoramus like myself in all their conversations. Indeed, they never made me feel an outsider and tried to explain their allusions when it was obvious that I was unable to follow the conversations.

Gradually, I became conscious of the august status of the company in which I found myself. At first it did not seem inappropriate to me that Arnold Toynbee or Gilbert Murray should be invited to put the sheets on my couch in the drawing room and make up my bed on those Sunday evenings when Mrs. Gubb was off duty. It was hard to appreciate the significance of these elderly gentlemen. They were simply Mrs. Hammond's old friends whom she had known because she had been one of the early generation of women students at Oxford's Lady Margaret Hall in 1892. She tried to entertain me with books that would tell me something of these visitors without burdening my mind with their scholarly productions. It seemed too difficult to ask her to explain their scholarship. So she brought me novels, many of which were written by Hammond friends and acquaintances from the shelves in one of the guest bedrooms. And when I had read Rosalind Murray's thinly disguised novel about her marriage to Arnold Toynbee, in which she made it clear that it was impossible to be married to "a saint," Barbara told me that Rosalind was Gilbert's daughter and had married and divorced Arnold Toynbee. Thereafter I looked with different eyes at Toynbee and his second wife, Veronica, who used to visit us together, and wondered how Veronica felt about living with a saint.

The visitors included a long string of names that I later came to recognize from various scholarly, political, or literary circles. A frequent guest, much appreciated by both of us, was Ruth Dalton, the wife of the recent Labor chancellor of the Exchequer.

By the time I met her, at the Hammonds' scrubbed kitchen table, Ruth was a member of the parks department of the London County Council and thus particularly interested in the history and development of London's open spaces. She spent many hours with Barbara and her manuscript in the revolving shelter on the lawn. Usually she came out from there deeply depressed as she felt that Barbara, at seventy-six, did not have the stamina or the will to continue with this work now that Lawrence was dead. Ruth and I sometimes talked about this problem, wondering whether perhaps Barbara had for so long depended on Lawrence's flair as a writer to interpret the material that she now felt inadequate to work on it herself. Ruth was kind and helpful to me. She invited me to visit her in London as soon as I was able to travel and continued to take a special interest in me and my affairs. Many years later I learned that she had lost her only daughter to a bone disease.

My favorite of all the visitors to Oatfield was Florence Halévy, the widow of Elie Halévy, the French historian of England. These two couples had been friends since the Hammonds had covered the Versailles Peace Conference in 1919 for the *Manchester Guardian*, and they had spent many long periods together. Florence was wonderfully warm and lively and, although she was Barbara's age, treated me as an equal. She implied that our common Continental background gave us an edge over Barbara's strange puritanical attitudes. A tall, elegant woman with a strong face and dark brown eyes, Florence felt undressed without the black velvet band around her long neck. She told me how, as a young woman, she had first been engaged to her husband Elie's brother, and how Elie had stolen her from him.

Florence Halévy was a racy raconteur and slightly irritated by Barbara's asceticism. She told me that she had always thought it deeply cruel and unnatural of Barbara to force Lawrence to sleep with her in that hideously cold and uncomfortable shelter. She could not bear it that Rags was always locked up in the bathroom when there was a bitch in heat in the neighborhood. "He should follow his instincts," she would tell Barbara, who simply smiled and kept Rags locked up. I was glad that Florence had never witnessed Rags's ecstatic raping of Veronica Toynbee's legs whenever she appeared at Oatfield. When I was able to move about more easily, without my crutches, Florence Halévy took me up to the National Gallery in London and lectured me on the lasciviousness of Zeus, illustrating his exploits with the paintings that surrounded us.

In between her visits to Oatfield, Florence wrote me long letters from her home, the Villa Halévy in Sucy-en-Brie near Paris, which had belonged to her father-in-law, Ludovic Halévy, the librettist of *Carmen*. In her letters Florence chivvied me to organize Barbara into getting on with her writing, which I was by then transferring onto the typewriter, and to make the domestic couple in the cottage more responsive to Barbara's needs. It was she who finally persuaded Barbara to give away Lawrence's clothes.

When, a little later during my convalescence, I was able to climb the stairs, Barbara showed me Lawrence Hammond's study on the first floor. This wonderful, light, rectangular room above the drawing room was furnished in a faded gray-green, with books lining the walls and dominated by William Rothenstein's large painting of a young Barbara sitting on a heather-covered hillside. With a mischievous smile, she pointed to her auburn hair in the painting. Fifty years later and now snowy white, it was still dressed in the same Edwardian fashion as a halo around her head. She did not wash it during the entire year of my time with her, but brushed it vigorously with one hundred strokes every night in the comfortable downstairs bathroom, while the cat purred loudly on his hot water bottle.

As we stood there meditating upon Rothenstein's painting, she told me that this was how she had looked at the turn of the century, when a disappointed young man composed the well-known doggerel about her academic achievements. And she recited it briskly:

I spent all my time with a crammer
and only could rise to a 'gamma.'
But the girl over there
with the flaming red hair
got an alpha plus easily—her!

Following in the footsteps of her oldest sister, Dorothy, one of eight student pioneers at Oxford's second college to open its doors to women in 1879, Barbara distinguished herself both academically and as captain of its hockey team and became one of its most renowned alumnae. She told me proudly that she was the first woman to bicycle through Oxford to her lectures in 1893 and how annoying she found the compulsory old lady chaperones who knitted stolidly through their tutorials.

The various visitors had by then given me an appreciation not only of the closeness of the Hammond marriage, but also of the extent of their joint scholarly creativity. It appeared that Barbara had done most of the research, going up to the British Museum regularly by train, and coming back with carefully prepared notes, while Lawrence used her notes to produce the books. Occasionally in a newspaper report or a book review someone would compare the Hammonds to that other couple who produced joint scholarly books—the Webbs. Such comparisons drove Barbara to tart sarcasm. She disliked the Webbs' cold statistics and personalities. Moreover, she objected to their having accepted a peerage, telling me how she and Lawrence had been offered a title some years previously, an honor they declined because they thought it incompatible with their belief in democracy. Aristocracy to Barbara smacked of the horsey set surrounding her in the country about Hemel Hempstead. Although she loved horses, and rode herself, that kind of horsiness she did not care for. I soon learned

Barbara's tolerance for any kind of music was very low, and, her fists banging on her thighs, she soon left the kitchen.

Sometimes Barbara spoke to me of her husband, whom, sadly, I had never met. She told me how wonderfully handsome she thought him when they first met at Oxford, but that she had grave doubts about his looks because he wore a splendid dark beard. What would he look like if it ever had to be shaved off? Did he have a chin? In fact it was shaved off some years after their marriage, and Barbara was much relieved to discover that indeed "he had a chin." I had quickly come to understand the strength and devotion of their relationship from the various table conversations of her guests, and even from the housekeeper's description of the occasion of his death. Lawrence had died in the late evening, and Barbara then sat alone by his side throughout the night, waiting until morning before she called for help.

Florence Halévy, however, sketched a slightly different picture of their relationship by suggesting that Barbara dominated the marriage and that it was her stubbornness and insistence on various household rules and matters of delicacy bordering on puritanism that made the menage at Oatfield as regimented concerning animals, sleeping arrangements, and food as it was.

An example of Barbara's attitudes is the occasion when a new young caretaking couple was installed some time after I had left Oatfield, the previous elderly couple, the Gubbs, having retired. Barbara was dreadfully upset when the husband came to tell her that his wife would have to go off to hospital to have her baby as her "waters had broken." She described this conversation to me as totally indelicate, repeating the phrase about "broken waters" in a voice of wonder and disgust.

Barbara was warm and welcoming to Gerry, whom she

to appreciate her distinctive mannerisms: the rhythmic banging of her fist against her thigh when she was agitated, and the extraordinary widening of her eyes when she was surprised or shocked, the dry little asides leveled at the "horsey set," and the allusions to the Webbs. In contrast to an honor from the crown, Barbara was extremely pleased with the honorary D. Litt. that Oxford University had bestowed upon herself and Lawrence and proudly showed me the photograph of them both marching in their academic robes at the time of the Encaenia.

I was amused by Barbara's political attitudes. In retrospect, I realized she was a socially conscious liberal of the late nineteenth century with a strong dose of Fabian asceticism. But she had a determination all her own, and Florence Halévy thought that, philosophically, Lawrence leaned far more to the left. Barbara destested the Tory "county" set in the neighborhood and dreaded an encounter with any of them. She was a spirited critic of all politicians and enjoyed being funny at their expense. Although she was extremely fond of Ruth, she could not abide Hugh Dalton, whose socialism and oratory she saw as pompous and hypocritical. But most of Barbara's mockery went against the philistinism of the right. She was also amused at the lack of sensitivity in diplomatic circles. She repeatedly delighted her listeners with the story of the famous historian R. H. Tawney's stint in the British Embassy in Washington, where no one knew how to place him, so that eventually he was classed with the typists. Tawney, whose speech at Lawrence's funeral Barbara treasured, was a close and cherished friend and figured often in her conversation.

Not only friends but also relatives came. Barbara's favorite niece, the poet Anne Ridler, was very welcome. But after she left, Barbara rolled her forget-me-not eyes and confessed that unfortunately she could not understand

Anne's poetry. I suspected that it was the religious ambience she could not understand or perhaps did not like. Anne's mother, Violet Bradby, who lived in nearby Little Gaddesden, an area that troubled Barbara as being too Tory, once brought me an anthology of poetry selected by General Wavell. "Can't think why Violet should think Wavell's selection should do anything for you!" was Barbara's comment when Violet had left. I was delighted with my present and didn't understand why I should not have been given it. Was it perhaps too Tory?

Another niece, Letty Chitty, a sparrowlike, unkempt woman, was a distinguished aeronautical engineer lecturing at Imperial College, who spent her free time collecting wildflowers in the mountains of Spain. I enjoyed Letty and was intrigued by her profession, but her forgetfulness and untidiness caused Barbara great concern. Somehow there was a cloud hanging over Barbara's sisters and perhaps herself, which was not clearly articulated. It seemed there was some fear of madness in the family. Another sister, nicknamed "Mick," had plagued the life out of Barbara when they were very small. The school grounds of Haileybury, where they lived while their father was headmaster, had a collection of pigs that were nurtured and then there was an annual pig slaughtering. When Barbara was about three, and Mick some eighteen months older, she convinced Barbara that she was not a girl at all but a pig. Moreover, when Barbara protested and said she would tell their parents, her sister assured her that the parents were bound to deny her porcine qualities, so that there was no point in asking them about it. She would simply have to live with the fact that she was indeed a pig. She would look at Barbara and grunt, twirl an imaginary tail and throw meaningful glances her way when the pigs could be heard.

Perhaps it was the memory of this deeply felt childhood terror, which Barbara admitted without any inhibition, that turned her into a quasivegetarian. She did eat fish and eggs but no meat. Apparently Lawrence had not shared her abhorrence of meat, and she was used to two separate main dishes being served at her table. Thus I and her other guests were offered as much variety of meat as the postwar rationing allowed, while our hostess lived mostly on cheese, eggs produced by obliging neighborhood farmers, vegetables, and the occasional fish. Except on the rarest occasions we all ate at the well-scrubbed bare wooden table in the comfortable kitchen surrounded by the permanently heated Aga stove and the coke hot water heater that needed twice daily stoking. The kitchen also boasted one comfortable armchair strictly reserved for the cat and red geraniums on the windowsill. I learned to distinguish Barbara's dearest friends from those less intimate according to where their meals were served. And although the dining room with the Rothenstein portrait of Lawrence Hammond was a pleasant room, I think all of us who were able to eat in the kitchen preferred its physical and emotional warmth.

It was the kitchen also that harbored the wireless to which we listened to the news and the serialized reading of Trollope's *Warden* and other classics. In the hospital I had become addicted to the soap opera *Mrs. Dale's Diary* and I now introduced Barbara to the daily afternoon installments of the drama of this middle-class doctor's wife. Years after I had left Oatfield, Barbara wrote to say that she was about to listen to *Mrs. Dale* and think of me. It was a most unlikely entertainment for her. She enjoyed the theater, and her London friends could easily persuade her to come and visit new exhibits at various art galleries. However, she seemed to be deaf to the delights of music. Whenever my friend Gerry came to stay at Oatfield, he was eager to listen to BBC concerts, but it was clear that

invited to stay over frequent weekends to keep me company. Gerry's conversational ability proved much more
adept than my own, and he kept up his end with intellectual
luminaries at the scrubbed kitchen table. Occasionally, he
was even asked to explain certain problems and theories of
physics and electronics and seemed to acquit himself reasonably well. Barbara left us to our own devices, and on sunny
afternoons we spent many pleasant hours in the field beside
the garden. But on one occasion, after I had moved to the
upstairs guest bedroom, I was already in bed in the early
evening with Gerry sitting by my side recounting some
amusing story, which made me laugh indecorously and too
loudly. Barbara rushed upstairs as though the house were
on fire and, with furious blazing eyes, demanded to know
why I had screamed. She clearly thought Gerry, that most
restrained of men, had assaulted me. Thereafter, I was
always most careful to lower my voice to a genteel English
murmur.

My mother, also, was invited to stay occasionally at
Oatfield as Barbara felt that we needed to see each other.
Well into her eighties my mother charmed everyone she
met, and her graciousness and presence now that she was
in her late forties did not fail at Oatfield. She was always
most generous to me and shared her earnings and any material possessions to make my physical life more comfortable.
But it was at this time, during my stay at Oatfield, that I
became interested in my relationship with her, although it
was not until much later that I began to consider her feelings toward me. Perhaps because Florence Halévy treated
me like a responsible adult, I now noticed my irritation at
my mother's desire still to mold me in some image that did
not suit my own ideas about myself. Well into my fifties
she could stir feelings of silent rage when she insisted on
telling me how to arrange my hair and which colors I
should wear. The fact that she was usually right in her

assessments was beside the point; I wanted to make my own decisions. But I can clearly remember occasions when I deliberately chose to thwart her protestations against minor points of my dress or deportment. Could I possibly have made some major decisions just to prove my rebelliousness? Certainly, my guilt feelings toward her are a prominent feature of our relationship. Guilt, possibly for not loving her enough, joined my fear of her anger for as long as I can remember. Just lately, I have wondered whether perhaps she also felt guilty about having "deserted" me when she had to make her own living away from me after our arrival in England. If so, her guilt was misplaced as my own at that time was due to my enjoyment of my new life and I felt that I ought to be missing her.

As the first year of my convalescence progressed, it was decided that I should do some work in Lawrence Hammond's study upstairs. So I was installed in that calm and inviting room with a typewriter. I divided my time between Gerry's Ph.D. dissertation, which was riddled with mathematical formulae and tables (some of which I calculated myself in order to complete the work on time) and Barbara's manuscript on the history of London's open spaces. Every so often Barbara went up to the British Museum by train, spending the day there, and returning exhausted in the evening. I was obviously far too unappreciative of her work, for she never described what she had been doing or how her struggles with this manuscript depressed her. She made a point of not boring me with the weight of her learning (I often wished she had), but when a huge box of the new paperback editions of the *Village Labourer* and the *Town Labourer* arrived, she presented me with copies, which I did not read with any understanding till some years later. My ignorance of her scholarship and the mechanics of research pained me because I felt instinctively that I would have enjoyed the ability to empathize with her problems and to enter more knowledgeably into the conversations with her friends. At the time, it did not in my wildest dreams occur to me that I might ever study, let alone be a historian myself. I knew already that I enjoyed the life of the senses—Barbara Hammond introduced me, if only vicariously, to the pleasures of the life of the mind.

EPILOGUE

CALIFORNIA

CHAPTER

8

ITT WAS TO TAKE TWELVE
years after my sojourn with Barbara Hammond came to an
end before I had the opportunity to develop the life of the
mind in any sustained and meaningful manner. When I left
her in 1950, my foot was healed, and, looking backwards,
I now realize that I could have done more or less anything
I wanted. At the time, however, my options seemed limited.
I felt obliged to follow the dictates of Gerry's generosity
and perhaps the commonly held fallacy that marriage would
give a young woman a certain amount of freedom. Gerry
had completed his degree and had faithfully and devotedly
kept up my spirits through my long and tedious illness.
Although I was emotionally unprepared for marriage, there
seemed to be nothing to prevent my acceptance of his pro-
posal. Had this happened in 1970 we would probably have
decided to live together. But it was 1950, and so I
exchanged my plaster cast for marriage.

Our ten years together were orchestrated by frequent
changes in domicile as we moved from England to New
York, from there to Connecticut, back to England, back

again across the Atlantic to Massachusetts and, finally, to California. These moves were never of my own volition, but to foster my husband's professional or career interests or his political convictions. For example, he was so deeply disturbed by the McCarthy atmosphere in the United States that we returned to England in 1952, and equally disturbed by the British role in the Suez Crisis so that we then returned to the United States in 1957. While I agreed with his political attitudes, I would not, if left to myself, have charged about the world. I felt that my whole life had been straddled between worlds, and I was eager to settle somewhere and to live among familiar people and scenery. By the time he wanted to move to California in 1959, I decided that by now I had had enough of this lack of stability and, if I was forced to move again, I would do so for my own reasons. We divorced and I re-married and settled, as I hoped for good, in an enchanted house overlooking a redwood grove in Woodside, California.

Before we left England for the United States, I had worked for five years in the public relations department of the government-sponsored New Town of Harlow in Essex. My fascinating job there was to settle new residents, to intervene in disputes between the architects, the planners, and the inhabitants of the town, and to introduce the stream of professional visitors (architects, journalists, politicians, health administrators) as well as potential residents to the idealistic dream we all had of this planned community. No position of such responsibility was even faintly possible in America without a university degree; I decided, with the enthusiastic and encouraging support of my husband, I would have to get one. Finding myself on the doorstep of Stanford University, I applied there to matriculate as a freshman at the age of thirty-six. Stanford, I hoped, would finally offer me the Oxford I had missed in England and the Charles University that I had missed in Prague.

It was now eighteen years since I had devoted my mind to sustained book-learning, and my high school education (in three English and three Czech schools) had been a grab bag of confused and unrelated bits and pieces. But I did have an Oxford School Certificate as well as a Czech University entrance certificate from Prague. In order to enroll as a student at Stanford, I was obliged to overcome a veritable obstacle course. First, I had to sit a college aptitude test in a huge hall full of adolescents all writing furiously. I waited several months to hear the results of this important first step. Apparently I had passed this test to the authorities' satisfaction. Then came the next hurdle. The Stanford registrar suggested that I be interviewed by professors of various departments, who might allow me a certain number of college credits for what I had supposedly learned during my high-school years, because a European high-school diploma was considered the equivalent of two years of an American college education. During the many months of preparation for these tests and interviews, I was in a perpetual state of stage fright. I remember this part of my whole educational venture as the worst time of all. I made the rounds of classics, French, German, mathematics, and chemistry discussing my hazy memories of high-school studies with learned gentlemen who wondered what I was doing there. Eventually I was informed that if I could maintain a B+ average during the first two terms, I would be absolved from two college years at Stanford; if not, I would have to work the usual four years to obtain a bachelor's degree.

My plan was to make a career of town, or, as it was called in the United States, city planning, having become fascinated by the subject during my work in England's Harlow New Town. As "city planning" was a graduate degree offered at the University of California at Berkeley, I intended to prepare myself for this in one of the social sciences as an undergraduate at Stanford.

I began my classes with great trepidation, surrounded by noisy and loquacious young students who appeared to know already everything we were supposed to be learning, and who were completely uninterested in discussing with me anything we were reading. They avoided me to the point of not acknowledging my presence when we met in the corridors. I understood that as I was obviously almost old enough to be their mother, someone from whom they had just managed to escape, I was not the most scintillating companion for them. I also observed some middle-aged women auditors in other courses who interrupted the professors to give the class the benefit of their personal experiences, and I vowed that I would never do this, as it quite rightly irritated academics and students alike. It did not even occur to me at the time that my personal history might be of interest to academic history classes as, following British tradition, I considered the twentieth century part of current affairs.

I would, however, have given a great deal to know how my fellow students reacted to our required readings. The reading itself was fascinating, but also very difficult. I had, of course, read constantly during my life, but I had always read for pleasure—now I was forced to read and remember it all so as to answer questions about the contents intelligently. I read extremely slowly. The students in my classes, I discovered, were able to swallow a whole book the night before the class, something that took me well over a week to digest. The most important course, obligatory for all freshmen, was a year of the history of "Western Civilization," which was mostly concerned with "Western thought." It consisted of weekly lectures by experts in the field and discussion groups three times a week with a young instructor. I found this course totally absorbing. Here were all the names of philosophers and writers I had heard about and never dared to approach. They, or rather the short pieces of their works that we were expected to read, were moreover quite manageable, and one could get at least a suspicion of what they thought.

One-third of the way through the first term we were expected to take our first "midterm" examination. I had read and re-read our assignments as well as various other books about the subject and went into the examination with the greatest feeling of dread. Once seated before the sheet of questions I tried to think of some original ideas. We had an hour for the exam, and all around me my fellow students were writing energetically, some of them filling the second little blue exercise book before I had managed to write half a page. By the end of the hour, I had squeezed out one and a half pages of one of those little blue books. I was sure I had failed and went home preparing myself for a lifetime as a typist.

Thank God, the young instructor who graded our examinations had found something of merit in my page and a half. He told me later that he kept turning the blue book around looking for a second one, not believing that I could possibly have written so little. But once he read what I had said he apparently understood that I did not realize that all that was expected of me was to regurgitate our assignments—and that I had indeed thought I was expected to produce an original idea about the decline of Greek civilization. In any case, he gave me an A-, and my college career was saved. I owe him a heavy debt of gratitude, not only for that A- but for making the course such a wonderful intellectual experience.

The courses in political science, the major subject that I had chosen as a preparation for city planning, were a deep disappointment. I realized fairly quickly that politics, and particularly the politics of American government, which I would have to deal with in any form of planning, were not only quite different from the possibly exaggerated, civilized memory I had of English civil service procedures, but downright painful to contemplate. I could not imagine myself part of the American political process—let alone on the side of planners dealing with an obstreperous American public determined to defy any kind of superimposed government plan. I found myself shying away from all thought of politics, but irresistibly drawn to any historical allusions in all political discussions.

Somehow I managed to keep up the necessary B+ average in my grades. However, by the end of the second term, the direction of my interest had firmly changed from political science to history, thanks to that compulsory and exhilarating year of thinking about the history of Western civilization. I determined to complete my undergraduate years studying history. I even occasionally commandeered Gerry Masteller, one of my freshmen classmates (who, in later years, became the owner of Palo Alto's most interesting bookstore, *Printer's Inc.*), to drink a cup of cocoa while I had a coffee in the student union and to talk about our studies. He went so far as to invite my husband and myself to his home to meet his family, and once in a while I had my entire "Western civ" discussion group to dinner at our house. By the second year I even met, in one of my undergraduate history courses, another woman student, Emily Thurber, who was almost as old as I and who became a lifelong friend. Generally speaking, however, while my classmates were frolicking on the beach or boating on the lake, I was doing the laundry, cooking dinner, and spending weeks writing and rewriting a term paper that they dashed off between midnight and breakfast during the night before it was due. Occasionally I would meet some classmate in the library stacks. I remember once, when I was particularly engrossed and enjoying the hunt for some elusive information that might clinch a point I was trying to make in a term paper, bumping into a handsome young premedical student from one of my history classes. He groaned about the boredom of the time spent in the stacks and said he couldn't wait to finish this part of his compulsory education.

As my fellow students were so diffident, I resorted to my family and friends with whom to discuss what I was learning. My husband read several of the books on my required reading list. And my friend Alma Kays and I began to have weekly lunches during which she listened patiently and enthusiastically to my undergraduate babblings. These occasions were intensely important to me as I was bursting with my new-found erudition.

It was during the second year of my history studies, when I was preoccupied with a course on nineteenth-century English history, in which the work of the Hammonds was becoming relevant to my readings, that Arnold Toynbee came to lecture to an overflow crowd requiring outside loudspeakers in the huge auditorium at the university. He invited me to have breakfast with him on the morning after his talk and there told me of Barbara Hammond's lingering and isolated end in the local hospital. It was painful to hear that her perspicacity and wonderful sense of irony had finally deserted her and that the mindless old age she had so dreaded had overtaken her in reality. But most of all it was sad to think of her being separated from the colors, the perfumes, and the peace of her beloved garden.

During the final term before graduation, and after another year in the libraries of Oxford, I produced a publishable research paper on an intriguing minor utopia written by an unfrocked German monk in the sixteenth century. The professor, Lew Spitz, under whose auspices I had begun to work on this topic, urged me to continue studying for a Ph.D. Knowing my slow working habits and the pressures of constant study, I was dubious about my ability to persevere with such an uphill effort, but, since history was clearly the most satisfying method of occupying one's mind, I eventually pulled myself together and sent in my application for graduate study.

I was now at the problematic age of thirty-nine. By the time I would begin graduate work, if accepted, I would be forty. So, thinking that no one would believe the proverbial thirty-nine on the application form, I wrote "forty." The rejection letter from the secretary of the history department's committee of graduate admissions was a blow, though not a mortal one. He wrote to point out that I was already at an advanced age, that by the time I had completed my graduate work I would be many years older, and that, unfortunately, the history department needed young blood to carry out its tasks. He emphasized also that the department had an age limit of thirty-five for beginning graduate study and that no exceptions could be made.

I telephoned my good friend and neighbor, Peg. She was busy, but she listened to my tale of woe and said, "You can brood about this for forty-eight hours, but then you must do something about it," and rang off. I got into my car and drove furiously up into the hills and walked about the splendidly wooded skyline, miles beyond the town, looking down onto the university's academic buildings and dominating red tower. I brooded, as Peg had advised, and my brooding went something like this: "These wretched old men with their white beards, how dare they say I am too old to study history? Surely there must have been someone in the history of Western civilization who began a worthwhile career after they were thirty-five years old? Wouldn't it be fun to find someone like that and write about him or preferably her?"

As I drove back down the hill, I began to formulate a way of finding my subject or subjects. I decided that I had the research material right there in my living room in the little bookcase harboring the *Encyclopaedia Britannica*. Within the next two weeks, I leafed through the twelve thick volumes of the *Britannica*, page by page, from A to Z, filling out reference cards for all the people who had begun in their mid-thirties or later whatever had produced enough fame to merit inclusion in this august reference work. I collected a satisfyingly large stack of cards and filled them with copious notes. The subjects ranged over a wide area of professions, geographic locations, and historical time periods. Having got the taste of this and finding it rather exciting, I next did the same with Peg's set of the *Encyclopaedia Americana*. Before I did so, however, I had already decided that there were far too many subjects for me to synthesize and that I had better narrow the range of subjects down to some manageable entity.

I had made my first discovery concerning women's history: a considerable number of those fitting my category were women—I therefore decided that I would concentrate on women only, and that is what I did with the *Americana*. There, I made my second interesting discovery concerning women's history: the place of women in history depends upon the attitude of the historian. I found that the *Americana* had included many more women than the *Britannica*, and that many of these additions were British women whom one would have expected to be discussed in the *Encyclopaedia Britannica*. Occasionally a woman included under her own name in the *Americana* would be hidden under the name of her "famous" brother, or father, or husband in the *Britannica*, but mostly the *Britannica* would omit her entirely. I began to suspect that Americans were more open to women's achievements than British scholars. I also began to appreciate how remarkable a man Lawrence Hammond must have been to have shared the title pages and spines of their books with his wife. Having exhausted the encyclopedias and also the dictionaries of national biography in the Stanford library, I began to read more about some of the women I had found who were particularly interesting. I also read these women's published letters, diaries, autobiographies, or fiction.

While I was thus occupied, I discovered that I was not alone in wanting to study at my advanced age. A group of Stanford faculty wives led by Yvette Gurley and Jing Lyman, the wife of my undergraduate history professor and adviser, Richard Lyman, decided that the university ought to be more sympathetic to part-time and older students. Knowing of my deep personal interest in this topic, Jing asked me to work with them. We arranged a meeting with various interested Stanford professors at the Alumni Association and tried to make our case for liberalizing Stanford's policies, particularly the university's discriminatory policies concerning age and part-time study. I made a passionate speech explaining how much more it meant to older students to be able to receive the benefit of a university education and how satisfying the acquisition of knowledge and the delights of research might be somewhat later in life than during the conventional time. The leaders of our group were determined to have Professor David Potter among the professors at this meeting, because they knew that he had written on women's place in American history, and they therefore expected him to be sympathetic to our cause. I was stunned when Potter announced unabashedly and without irony that he saw his graduate students as apprentices to be trained to continue his own ideas and that middle-aged women were unsuitable for this task as they had too many ideas of their own. A little later I heard Potter lecture on women's historical contribution to American society. By now I was not surprised by his argument that while women had been producers during the Colonial period of American history, by the twentieth century they had turned into consumers, and in this way they contributed adequately to society. In looking around the audience, I saw the dissatisfaction with this argument on the faces of most women students and was glad to hear him challenged by a young blond student, Karen Offen, whom I later came to know well.

As part of my work for the group led by Jing Lyman and Yvette Gurley, I made it my business to survey the San Francisco Bay Area's colleges and universities to find out what opportunities they offered to older or part-time students. We then published a small pamphlet on my findings, but I also profited personally by discovering that the University of Santa Clara would allow me to study for an M.A. degree without worrying unduly about my advanced age. They liberally allowed me to arrange my own curriculum in part, and I decided to read what I could find on women's history. So it was that I spent the next two years more or less with directed reading concentrating on women in European and British history.

This effort was no easy task in the late 1960s, when one had to dig quite hard to find a few nuggets of information buried far and wide among millions of historical tomes that never mentioned a woman or women's concerns. I decided to try to replicate some of my undergraduate, Western civilization readings, but this time I would see what these great thinkers of the past had to say about women. To begin with I tried the Old and New Testaments, Aristotle, and Augustine. Almost immediately, I made my third important discovery concerning women's history, and I was shocked and dismayed. These renowned thinkers upon whom our civilization was based had by and large an appalling view of women. Aristotle claimed that woman was a failed man; St. Paul said man was the head of woman. I began to read more widely in later periods and found that women had very uneven political and legal rights, that they had been subservient to men, and that the laws of marriage and divorce had favored men as had education and economics in past centuries.

It is usually held that the racial and student turmoil of the late 1960s produced the new wave of feminism, and it is asserted almost invariably that the new interest in women's history was the result of this new militancy. This is categorically not my experience. Occasionally Betty Friedan's work *The Feminine Mystique* is given credit for the new feminism. But at the time of Friedan's book, I was by no means an imprisoned housewife—I was enjoying my undergraduate studies; and at the time of the student unrest in the late sixties, I was deep in my own historical research. My involvement with feminist ideas came purely from my historical studies. The more I read, the more I became convinced not only of the unevenness of men's and women's progress through history, and therefore through life, but also of the cyclical attempts by women to improve their own situation and the barriers that were then cast in their way.

I found, however, that there were also outstanding beacons in the bleakness of women's position. Plato suggested that men and women should rule jointly; as early as 1400, the French poet Christine de Pizan insisted that boys and girls should be educated equally and demonstrated a strong awareness of the inequities of women's historical treatment. During several specific periods, that is periods of what one might call feminist awareness, a number of historians occupied themselves with the history of women. These historical periods stood out quite clearly in my solitary reading: one of them was the Renaissance; another was the time just after the French Revolution; and a third was during the 1920s, just after women had won their battle for suffrage in several Western nations. Much later I worked out that these periods of awareness by historians coincided with failed or successful attempts by women to improve their situation.

I enjoyed my independent studies immensely. I think I must have bored my professors to tears with my enthusiasm for the people and ideas I discovered. I talked about them endlessly both during my official discussion sessions and on those occasions when they invited me to lunch in the university's faculty club.

When it came to choosing a topic for an M.A thesis, I was able to make use of my researches into the encyclopedias and wrote on four intellectual nineteenth-century British late starters who had made major contributions both to science and to literature without the benefit of structured and institutionalized higher education. The scientists were Caroline Herschel and Mary Somerville; the writers, Frances Trollope and Elizabeth Gaskell. I was able to put these women's lives into some historical context through my general historical reading on women during the previous two years. For example, two of my subjects, the mathematician, Mary Somerville, and the writer, Frances Trollope, had financially supported their husbands and children with the earnings they produced through their intellectual endeavors, at a time when women's earnings legally belonged to their husbands. Elizabeth Gaskell, another of my subjects, had signed the parliamentary petition urging the passage of the Married Women's Property Act, which finally put an end to this practice.

I remember one of the three male examiners who discussed my thesis with me wanting to know whether Mrs. Gaskell was a "feminist" and the problem this question posed on that occasion in 1970. Two decades later, the issue of what constitutes "a feminist" and "feminism," both during a specific historical period and today, is still unresolved and fiercely debated, both at scholarly meetings, and in the academic literature. In 1850 Elizabeth Gaskell wanted control of her own earnings and was willing to sign petitions to change the law to make this possible. She was pretty annoyed with her husband for "composedly buttoning up" her money in his pocket and doling out to her only what he thought she needed or wanted to give to charity. She admired John Stuart Mill, whom most nineteenth-century adherents of "feminism" throughout Europe and America, at that time, considered their leading exponent. She longed for "an independent inner life," yet she believed that motherhood was the "greatest and highest duty" of all women and that an independent inner life must not interfere with this duty. These views set her fairly well into the "feminist" context of the mid-nineteenth century, but would not necessarily have made her a feminist by the standards of 1970.

When I had completed these two years and my M.A. was in hand, I discussed with Matt Meier, the chair of Santa Clara's history department, what I should now do with my acquired knowledge of women's history. It certainly did not occur to me that I might teach, but I vaguely hoped to write. Matt surprised me by suggesting that I offer a course on women's history to one of the local community colleges. I suppose he thought that, since I had talked endlessly about my wonderful discoveries to the assembled history faculty, I might just as well talk about them to students. I was lucky in finding a ready market for this idea at Cañada College near my home, at a time when teaching women's history was but a gleam in a very few people's eyes. Through Cañada College I taught my first course to a group of forty women. Among them was one trio made up of three generations of the same family—grandmother, mother, and daughter. It was a course never to be forgotten, both for my own enthusiasm and for that of the students. Although I have taught many similar courses since then, that particular course, as one of my students said, was like a successful honeymoon and everything shone.

In order to give the students something to read, I had made a collection extracted from the many volumes I had waded through to find even a few short paragraphs dealing with women. In due course, I was able to publish a revised and extended version of this collection under the title *Women from the Greeks to the French Revolution*, a text aimed at students who know little about the context of these centuries. While working on this text, I remembered the bored footballers during my own year as a student of the history of Western civilization, and how they had always come to life when the subject matter turned to sport. I had thought then, if only one could teach a course on the history of "sport in Western civ," many unwilling students would be turned around. Now I was doing just that by looking at women in "Western civ," but fortunately my students were anything but unwilling—they were entranced.

Nevertheless, I quickly became aware that the students knew very little about the history of the times I was covering and I thought how useful it would be if I could show contemporary pictures of the historical figures. I even thought of coming to class in costume, but finally settled on making slides from art, using my husband's technique and camera, to illustrate my ideas. Eventually I was able to lecture on many occasions with these slides, usually just before the final exams, to remind the students of the discussions we had had throughout the term.

In 1971 the historian Natalie Davis, recently arrived at Berkeley, urged me to attend the meeting of the Western Association of Women Historians, which assembled once a year at a quiet retreat on the coast south of Santa Cruz. I was hesitant since my education had been so unorthodox and I doubted my ability to communicate with this group. But Natalie insisted. "They will like what you are doing," she said. So I went. The group consisted of about sixty women historians gathered from all areas of California and from as far away as Seattle and Arizona. We talked all day and much of the night and walked for long periods on the beach among the sweet perfume of the ice plant–covered escarpment. The meeting was a milestone in my life both because it was wonderful to meet so many people who shared my interests and also because their encouragement spurred me to ever more interesting and ambitious plans of work. I shall always be grateful to this organization for its generous helpfulness and especially for its informality.

One of the women at this gathering was intrigued when I mentioned that I had made slides to illustrate my lectures on women's history. She asked whether I could show some of these slides to the group. I phoned home, and my husband arranged to have all my slides and the projector sent down to Santa Cruz. Then I stayed awake throughout the entire night in that monastic room, thinking out a coherent talk that would incorporate as many of my three thousand slides as possible to show the technique I had developed for illustrating historical points with pictures taken from the art of the period. I was extremely nervous as, like all novices, I assumed that everyone must know far more than I did about the subject. When, the next evening, I gave my slide talk, I was astonished to discover that for most of those present what I had to say was completely fresh and surprising. The boost to my confidence was enormous. I made many new friends and promptly acquired a widespread net of a likeminded community who invited me to speak to their classes in San Francisco, in San Diego, in Los Angeles, and to stay in their homes. It was a heady new life.

During these years, I also worked intermittently on developing some essays on the individual late starters I had found in my search through the encyclopedias. The person who appealed to me most was Christine de Pizan, the fourteenth-century French poet and author who wrote that at the age of thirty-five she had sat herself down like a child learning its ABC and had begun to study the classics of history and philosophy. I had noticed her name as the only woman to appear in a course on the Renaissance I had taken in my undergraduate years, when Huizinga cited her briefly in his *Waning of the Middle Ages*. I had found some glowing jewellike medieval illuminations in her manuscripts that I used in my slide lectures to elucidate the lives of women at that time. She had also written two works on the position of women in 1405, which, when I found them, had not yet been translated into English, and they intrigued me immensely by their hardheaded and unsentimental practicality. I spoke often about Christine de Pizan in my classes and hoped to be able to write something about her.

The occasion to do so arose when Karen Offen suggested that I should write a paper on Christine de Pizan's ideas on education, and that, together with Stanford's early modern historian, Carolyn Lougee, we should present a panel on three stages of education in France at the 1973 American Historical Association's meeting in San Francisco. That meeting, my first official appearance at this vast collection of thousands of historians, was a terrifying but also most happy and satisfying experience. Just before our session, I was waiting in the lunch queue of the huge conference hotel wishing I had someone with me to calm my nervousness, when a young woman standing in front of me peered at my name tag and became very excited as she knew my book *Women from the Greeks to the French Revolution*. She introduced herself as Marian Horowitz and told me that she was using my book as a text in a course she taught

in Massachusetts. That chance encounter did wonders for
my morale, as did the crowded room at our session. I discovered later that a large number of the audience were there
because they also knew my book.

I had met Karen Offen a couple of years earlier when
she came to listen to one of my community college classes
at the Holbrook Palmer Mansion in Atherton. Unfortunately, she had also brought her nine-month-old daughter,
Catherine, who amused herself by crawling around the
room twanging the door stops during my lecture. While
I was sympathetic to the problems of women who were
housebound with small children and needed to continue
with their professions, I was eventually forced to expel both
mother and child from the room. Some of the older women
in this class muttered furiously that they had been forced
to stay home with their small children for years and now
finally had the opportunity to widen their horizons. They
felt it was unfair of young women like Karen to want to
have it all and thereby spoil their chance by bringing a
noisy child into the class. Nevertheless, Karen and I were
drawn together by our mutual interests and went on from
that time, becoming both friends and colleagues, and in due
course I invited her to work with me on the two-volume
book that the Stanford University Press was to publish in
1983 under the title *Women, the Family, and Freedom,
1750–1950*.

In this work, we decided to demonstrate, with as many
original texts as possible, the vigorous debate about women.
We traced the debate as it raged through two centuries
both nationally and internationally. We translated French
and German contributions to the debate when necessary
and called on our friendly experts in other languages to
help with Italian, Norwegian, and Russian. We placed the
debate into its historical, political, socio-economic, and artistic contexts. We concluded that whenever women joined

general movements for political liberty or educational/economic opportunities and then wanted to apply these movements' manifestos to themselves, the "nature of woman" (always described as either too weak or too moral) made such changes in women's status inadmissible. Powerful male experts and institutions relentlessly insisted that such changes were not in society's, or even in women's own, interest.

One day in 1974, soon after I had returned from the famous second meeting of the Berkshire Conference on Women's History at Radcliffe and Harvard University, the telephone rang. The caller was Glenna Matthews, one of Stanford's history graduate students. She said, "I have been delegated to invite you to speak at a conference on 'Teaching Women's History,' which the Stanford history department is planning to hold on January twenty-fifth next year. Professor Degler wants to see your slides and what you do with them." I could hardly believe my ears. Degler was the man best known in the field of American women's history at that time. He had come to Stanford after my application for graduate admission had been rejected by the department. I must have answered fairly coherently because we settled on the topic for my talk and arranged that I would be the first speaker of the conference.

When I stood on the stage of Bishop Auditorium, giving the history department the benefit of my self-taught knowledge and experience, it was a piquant moment, enhanced by the fact that the day of the meeting was my birthday. It was now exactly ten years after that fateful year when I was supposedly over the hill and too old to study history.

The more I read and puzzle about historical connections, the more I have become convinced that history is a vital clue to understanding our lives. The lack of knowledge and understanding of the past sometimes seems like a deliberate unwillingness to know. It is surely a waste of human energy for new generations to fight old battles over and over again. I have been eager to emphasize this issue ever since my earliest study of women's history. Historical blindness seems, however, to be a human character flaw and applies not only to the deeply entrenched relationship between the sexes. As I know to my cost, religious, racial, and ethnic groups are equally and relentlessly anchored in their own values and certainties, boasting an ugly chauvinism that hinders peaceful coexistence among people.

As I write this, in 1990, the Iron Curtain has been rent, the Berlin Wall dismantled, and the unification of the two Germanys is taking place. One of the further issues, once again, is the unlikely possibility of carving the Sudetenland out of Czechoslovakia and incorporating it into a new combination of German-speaking peoples. Some Sudeten Germans, who were expelled or decided to remove themselves to either of the Germanys after 1945, are still demanding to return to their "homeland" almost fifty years later. It seems hard to believe that people cannot grasp the two most significant truths about that little word *home*. The first, as I discovered quite painfully, is simply that one can't go home again: people change, places change, and what one remembers is often a mirage. The second is that home is not so much a physical place but a concept of the mind and, perhaps, a community in which one is at ease, a concept or a community that we must forge for ourselves—no one else can create it for us.

But perhaps it is wrong to be impatient with those who find it hard to understand, because I too have learned these lessons infinitely slowly, over a lifetime since Hitler and an embarrassed Sudeten German headmaster told a young girl that her presence was no longer desired in their school. Gradually I discovered that I could not identify with any nation, race, or religion. I have lived in Czechoslovakia, in both the Sudetenland and the heartland of Czech Bohemia in Prague; I have lived in England; and I have lived in the United States. I have been, and could be, a legal citizen of any of these countries and hold passports for all of them. As a child I have also been officially affiliated with Lutheranism and Anglicanism, and my ancestors were Jews. I have thus been unusually fortunate to have had numerous possibilities to create an identity for myself and even to choose which one I would like to consider as primary. But I have also been a German among Czechs, a Continental among Britons, a European among Americans, a Protestant among Jews, and a Jew among Gentiles. So, although I have obviously taken some facets of all of them into myself, I cannot choose any one of these identities above any other, partly because they did not choose me, but mostly because I believe that ethnic, religious, or racial identities are obliged to adopt or accept certain values that are potentially xenophobic.

There is, nevertheless, one identity about which there is no question—I was not able to choose it, I have no desire to change it, and it seems unlikely that anyone will expel me from it: I am human—but a woman. My historical studies have made me aware of the injustices done to humanity over centuries by preventing women from developing their full potential. Therefore, like everyone who is willing to consider and to understand the past, I cannot help but be a feminist—that is, to work towards putting this right. Through my work as a historian, I have found likeminded spirits of women and men, in many parts of the world, who offer a community (and a home) that is more tolerant than any of those other groups to whom I find it so hard to relate. But even here in this welcoming community of the spirit, it seems to be important, constantly, to guard against exclusiveness and prejudice as those frightening, unyielding tendencies that have produced ethnic, religious, and sexual chauvinism lurk in us all.

Over the years, then, it has slowly but ever more insistently become clear to me that a friendly community may offer a wide and comforting safety net of likeminded spirits; that close and loving friendships enhance life a thousandfold; but that none of these will provide a home if one does not have the inner strength to think and to be alone.